DEATH AND THE GENTLE BULL

Death and the Gentle Bull

(A Captain Heimrich Mystery)

BY

RICHARD AND FRANCES LOCKRIDGE

J. B. LIPPINCOTT COMPANY

Philadelphia *New York*

PRINTED IN THE UNITED STATES OF AMERICA

LIBRARY OF CONGRESS CATALOGUE CARD NUMBER 54–6111

To Giff and Fletch Cochran
and to their
International Grand Champion,
Ankonian 3216th,
who permits himself to be prodded by admirers

DEATH AND THE GENTLE BULL

I

THE HOUSE ITSELF was on a rise. Cars climbed from the road to it, along a drive shaded by tall hemlocks. People left the cars and went through the house, which was cool and empty; went through french doors, across a flagged terrace, to the lawn, which was by no means empty—nor, indeed, noticeably cool. People who were unfamiliar with Deep Meadow paused on the terrace and, according to their natures, gave forth small gasps of wonderment, audible yelps of the same or merely blinked their eyes. Evelyn Merritt, although she had seen it often, caught her breath and Wade Landcraft smiled down at her and nodded and said it would be even better in the spring, with pink and yellow and the faintest of greens on the hills.

Bonita Landcraft, on the other hand, said, "My God, Harv! I still don't believe it! I'll *never* believe it. It's painted on. Somebody *painted* it on." To which Harvey Landcraft said, yes, it was quite a view, and then, "The bar's usually over there," indicating. The bar was; the bar was part of the foreground. A long buffet table was part of the foreground; round tables under bright umbrellas were part of the foreground; some hundred and fifty people, in shade and in shadow, were part of the foreground. So were two busy photographers. "She does a nice job," Harvey Landcraft said. "Come on, Bonny."

The lawn lay level for two hundred feet or more beyond the terrace. Then green land began gently to descend from the ridge, toward the white barns a thousand feet away. Beyond and to either side of the white barns were paddocks and pasture land lower still. A large tent was half hidden by one of the barns. Through the fields a sparkling small stream ran, and could be seen from the terrace. And beyond the valley, green hills rose in a kind of mannered turbulence against the sky. There was even a prettily innocent white cloud above one of the hills, obviously, Bonita Landcraft reflected, tethered there for the occasion.

Margaret Landcraft, although she continued to listen to a smallish man, whose face a little resembled a potato left too long in the baking oven, considered the cloud. It did not, she hoped, presage a break in the weather. Bad weather rendered people less expansive, more inclined to fault finding. On the day of The Sale it was, naturally, best to have people as expansive as they could be got. Well, Alec professed confidence that tomorrow would be fine and it had to be admitted that he was good about weather. Better than the Weather Bureau, for all the money "they" spent on it.

"It's such a beautiful place," Evelyn Merritt said. "So really beautiful."

"And on the other hand," Wade said, "it does smell of cows, doesn't it?"

Evelyn sniffed.

"It's hardly noticeable," she said, so admitting that it was a little noticeable. A gentle breeze blew upward from the barns, which lay to southwest of the house. The breeze was, undeniably, tinged with the not unpleasant, somewhat ammonic, scent of cattle habitation. It was not, Evelyn thought, really worth mentioning.

"Not to them, anyway," Wade said, and waggled a long finger at the people on the lawn. "It's the air they breathe."

"Naturally enough," Evelyn said, and was agreed with, almost too emphatically.

"It gets into the pores," Wade said.

Evelyn Merritt said, "Nonsense," almost sharply, and Wade looked down at her. Then he smiled. She was slight; she had deeply red hair, cut short. (As if, he thought, to minimize its richness.) She had blue eyes. But her skin did not redden in the sun, or too much freckle. She had a kind of golden tan, now in mid-September—golden tan on face and neck and arms. And (he glanced lower, in appreciation) on slim, un-stockinged legs.

"We," Evelyn said, but did not hurry it, "we are blocking traffic." She put a hand on his arm, let it rest a second, removed it. "A nice, long drink," she said. "With a great deal of ice."

They walked, side by side, across grass which seemed to welcome their feet. He was dressed as were most of the other men, in tweed jacket and grayish slacks and a colored shirt; he was as brown as the other men, with that special deepness of coloration which persists when there are no bleaching winters in a city; about his gray eyes there were those small crinkles which come from being much in the sun. He was even beginning, now in his late twenties, to develop the somewhat heavy shoulder muscles of a man who does country work. (He could swing her off the ground and into his arms with, apparently, no effort to speak of.) As they walked among Margaret Landcraft's guests, gathered for the traditional buffet which preceded The Sale, he was in no sense alien.

But for all that, Evelyn thought, he's not a countryman and never will be. He's not a cattle man, and won't be. He's not in his place; not really in his place. Some day he would be Deep Meadow Farm, since there was no likelihood that Harvey would want more to do with it than (naturally) his proper share of its profits. Wade would be going to the shows in the east, and in the west—to Chicago, to Kansas City—as his mother went now. He would show the Aberdeen Angus of Deep Meadow Farm, and know as much as most about the breed, and about its breeding. It was too late for him to start over. At least—

They had stopped while Wade talked to a man from Omaha, about Deep Meadow Prince. Wade was saying, lightly, pleasantly, that he didn't doubt it; that Mr. Burns, from Omaha, was not alone. Prince would be an addition to anybody's herd of beef animals. Wade shook his head. "I doubt if you could get mother to set a price," he said. "Any price at all."

At least, it would be too late in another year or two, in another five at most. He had not yet quite acquiesced; now—today, tomorrow, next week, next month—he might well chuck it and start over. He wasn't clear, admitted he wasn't clear, at what. He didn't know what else he'd be good at. "And" (he had said, more than once) "at this I'm all right, Evvie. No great shakes, but good enough. What else—" He had shrugged. He had once wanted to be an architect. He was not sure that he any longer much wanted that. He wasn't sure what he wanted.

"Probably nothing enough any more," he said. "Except—" He had pointed, then, aiming his right index finger as he might a weapon, and at her breast.

Well, she thought, as they walked toward the trestle table with the two men in white jackets behind it—well, her he had, would always have. They would marry—how long was it, now? Two weeks from yesterday they would marry and, it was to be hoped, live happily ever after in a place of beauty, after all only pleasantly aromatic of Aberdeen Angus. Which would be all right with her, if with him. If, finally, he could acquiesce without bitterness, it would not matter. The cattle were pleasant creatures.

They had stopped again; a host had duties. She looked out toward the pastures, bright in the slanting sun. Black cattle seemed to float in the green grass. It was remarkable how nearly legless the Angus breed had become. It was, in a fashion, rather endearing. It would be fine here, with Wade—even with Wade and Wade's mother. Her mind slightly accentuated the qualifying phrase. She regretted this. Mrs. Landcraft was admirable in all respects—if a little formidable, if somewhat—well, "absorbing" was perhaps as good a word as any. But Evelyn Merritt, to become Evelyn Landcraft in thirteen days, had no thought that she would be herself absorbed. Everything could, she was certain, be made to jog along most comfortably. They would—she stopped herself. She had been about to think they would grow old gracefully. It was an odd solace to find at the age of twenty-four. It was odd to seek solace at twenty-four.

They started on again, still toward the trestle table with bottles on it, with glasses catching the slanting sunlight, with two white-coated, active men. There were several groups near the bar; Bonita and Harvey formed a group of two. How inevitably, Evelyn thought, Bonita Landcraft carried New York with her—even here, with country spread so widely, so greenly, Bonita might have been standing on pavements. She was standing very prettily, to be sure. Grass did not seem actually to perturb her.

Bonita flicked a hand in greeting. She said, "Hi, you two," and Harvey turned, at her words, and raised his right hand in something like a salute. He did not really look a great deal like Wade—for one thing, he was new enough to the sun to have a sunburned nose. The facial contours were different, the mouth different, the body heavier. About his gray eyes there were no sun crinkles; the eyes themselves seemed quicker, shrewder.

"Hello," Evelyn said and Wade said, "'Lo Bonny. Harv. Been here long?"

Harvey Landcraft looked at his glass. He said, "About half a drink." He looked at Evelyn. He said, "Hi, sister-in-law." He looked around the lawn. The caterer's men had begun to arrange food on the buffet table. "She's really going to town this time," Harvey Landcraft told his brother.

"It's a big sale," Wade said. "Her biggest. A party even *Life* attends." He indicated the busy men with cameras.

"And this—" Harvey waved his hand at "this"—"softens them up. Does it, do you suppose?"

He did not seem to expect an answer; from his brother he got a shrug. "I'll get us something," Wade said. "Gin and tonic? Scotch, bourbon, rye?"

"Gin and tonic," Evelyn said. "In a very tall glass." Wade went. Evelyn smiled at Bonita Landcraft. She said, "You look cool."

"Oh," Bonita said. "I am, as a matter of fact. Within reason."

It was enviable, Evelyn thought, still smiling. It was unquestionably true. It was not only the white dress, although the white dress helped. (And what it must have cost! Evelyn Merritt thought.) It was Bonita herself; so slenderly trim and poised, feather-cut brown hair so artfully disarranged. Evelyn was conscious that her own forehead was faintly moist.

"For some reason," Bonita said, "I'm sort of air-conditioned. Look—does it smell of cows?"

"A little," Evelyn said.

"Good," Bonita said. "I thought maybe I was smelling things. It's not a bad smell, really."

"No."

"Aberdeen Number Five," Harvey Landcraft told them both. "Ready for another, Bonny?"

Bonita was not. Harvey looked at his glass in reproach. He said, "Excuse me, ladies," and went toward the bar.

"Madison Avenue thirst," Bonny said. "Do you think mine's getting a little fat?" They looked at the trestle table, where the brothers were side by side. "Yours isn't," Bonny said. "Depends on the kind of bull you throw, apparently."

"Harvey looks fine," Evelyn said.

"As a matter of fact, he is. But there's no point in letting him know, is there?" She appeared to consider. "Of course," she said, "I do. Let him know, that is. You do yours?"

"Oh yes," Evelyn said. "It's hard not to, isn't it?"

"You know," Bonita said, "I've never tried much. Not for a long time, anyway. They're big bastards, aren't they?" A third man had joined the Landcraft brothers. "Not that he won't let you die of thirst," Bonita said. "Come on. We're heifers on our own, apparently." She put a hand on one of Evelyn's slim brown arms. "I'm glad Wade found you, if it's all right to say so. Or was it the other way round?"

"Either way," Evelyn said. "Both ways, I guess."

"So long," Bonita said, "as mamma didn't enter in. I take it she didn't?"

"No."

"She does, you know. If allowed. One has—well, to put up signs. Private property, keep off. You know?" She looked at Evelyn. "I see you do," she said, although Evelyn said nothing. Bonita suddenly linked her arm in Evelyn's. "Heifers of the world, unite," she said. "To the bar, *march!*"

They went, arm in arm, red head and brown head at a level, tanned slim legs in cadence.

"Now there," Alec Ballard said to the man next him. "There go a couple of real baby dolls. The boys do themselves well."

"Very."

They continued for a moment to watch the girls. Then Ballard turned back to the shorter man. He said, "Well?"

"I'll think about it," the other man said. "When there's anything to think about. All you say is 'if.' "

"That's right," Ballard said. "Nothing sure about it. But you'd be interested. A lot would."

"Oh," the other man said. "Interested. Yes. But I know Margaret."

"Sure you do. Sure you do. She knows you too, doesn't she? Eh?"

The other man looked at Ballard. He had to look up. Alec Ballard was tall; a heavy, powerful man. He's a little like a bull himself, the other man thought.

"We've known each other for some years," he said, mildly. "Join me for a drink?"

"Better circulate," Ballard said. "She expects it, you know."

"As you like," Arnold Thayer said.

"As I'm told's more like it," Ballard said. He went off. The smaller man looked after him. Very like a bull, Thayer thought. Or did he plan to seem so? Thayer went toward the bar.

If Arnold Thayer thought he could go behind her back, he would have opportunity to think again. Margaret Landcraft noted this obvious fact in passing, while she said, "Other end, man. Take advantage of what wind there is, for God's sake," to the one of the caterer's men who was setting up a pedestal fan at an end—the wrong end, of course—of the buffet table. The fan, very large, leashed by fifty feet of flex to an outlet on the terrace, was intended to discourage flies, providing a headwind. (Or, depending on the flies, a tail wind.) There would be flies all the same; flies were a part of nature; on a stock farm they sometimes seem the largest part of nature. There was one now on one of the turkeys. Well, the people here tonight were used to flies.

Mrs. Landcraft looked across the turkey—and the hams,

the cold roasts of beef, the bowls of salad, the hooded brazier in which hot dishes were being kept tepid—and regarded, from some distance, her daughter-in-law and her daughter-in-law-to-be. Like all of them nowadays, Mrs. Landcraft thought, they dressed to be looked at. No wonder they were. Especially that-wife-of-Harvey's. Bonita—of all the improbable names! What kind of parents would they be who named a girl Bonita? With a name like that, they had only themselves to blame if she turned out no better than she should be; turned out, specifically, to be in the chorus of a television musical, with the legs—of which she so evidently was proud—visible in their entirety to anyone who could turn a knob.

Bonita turned from the bar, standing so that the westering sun was behind her. Nothing, so far as Margaret Landcraft could see, under that skimpy white dress. And with the light slanting as it did, Margaret Landcraft could see enough—too much. Her own son's wife! Her *oldest* son's wife! The wife of the son who should be, and who wasn't, devoting himself to Deep Meadow Farm. Mrs. Landcraft shook her head—apparently at the turkey. What a disappointment Harvey was!

Evelyn wasn't, or didn't seem to be, quite so bad. She wasn't wearing many more clothes, but nowadays none of them did. Her name was not one Mrs. Landcraft would have chosen but, at least, it was better than Bonita. ("Bonny," of all things!) And the Merritts were a good enough family; a family with roots. Not as long in Putnam County as the Landcrafts, naturally. That would have been too much to expect. And certainly not as long as the Wades, who had been there since the Revolution. (And of whom Margaret Landcraft appeared to be the last. Her brother was married and childless; he was also close to seventy, so that little was to be expected.)

If Wade, in whom the name continued to live, although misplaced—if Wade had to get married, he could have done worse, perhaps. This girl of his was flighty now, but she would—at least, one could hope she would—settle down. She'd never take a real interest in the herd, probably. But Wade didn't either. That Margaret Landcraft faced, as she had for several years. What would happen to Deep Meadow when she died hardly bore thinking of.

Margaret Landcraft thought of it only briefly. She was sixty-two, but what was sixty-two, when one lived a healthy life out of doors, and kept up one's interests? Sixty-two was an age at which men became presidents of the United States, and of large corporations. Obviously, women, who notoriously lived longer than men, had no reason, at sixty-two, to feel older than middle-aged. Grandfather Wade had lived into his nineties—and been as cantankerous as ever to the end.

Margaret said, "There, man!" pointing, to a waiter who could not, although he was looking directly at it, see the unoccupied table space which would easily accommodate the bowl he carried.

"Everything's ready now, Mrs. Landcraft," Mr. Pringle, who was supervising the catering in person, said from behind her.

"See it is," Mrs. Landcraft said. "Tell them. Not that some of them won't drink half the night anyway."

She went around the table, moved toward the area of the bar, where the population was most concentrated.

"She bears down," Bonita told Evelyn. "She's been glaring at us for minutes, you know."

"Yes," Evelyn said. "Perhaps she was just—abstracted."

Bonita Landcraft made a small sound, not distant from a snort.

"Not her," Bonita said. "Not she. She's been saying to herself, 'That-wife-of-his.' She's been thinking how she'd love to get something on me—something really juicy, something that would open Harv's eyes. Don't I know!"

"I suppose she is a little like that," Evelyn said. "She—"

"A little!" Bonita could not wait to say it. "A little? Watch yourself, lady. You've had warning—more than I had. Don't sell mamma short. For heaven's sake—*look at her!*"

Evelyn did, literally, although knowing Bonita had intended more.

Margaret Landcraft was beyond doubt formidable. She strode toward them. She's as tall as Wade, Evelyn Merritt thought. Why does she wear that dress?

The dress was pinkish; it probably was pink linen; it had been, conceivably, intended as a golf dress. It was, alarmingly, alien to the woman who wore it. From its sleeves—which were of precisely the wrong length—muscle-corded arms projected as if they sought escape. Above its round collar, which under other circumstances might have appeared demure, Mrs. Landcraft continued—neck as muscular as arms, long face long-weathered, gray hair cut short, cut almost in a masculine brush. Formidable, almost masculine and yet—no, by no means masculine. The sinewy arms depended from a body which, in hearty curves, was as feminine as a body might well be. And Mrs. Landcraft's legs—stockinged in the heaviest of nylon, feet shod for utility—were as smoothly contoured as a girl's and, unexpectedly, as slender.

"She must have been very handsome when she was younger," Evelyn said.

"In a large way," Bonita said, and then grinned suddenly, with unexpected frankness. "Yes, I'll give her that. However it hurts, I'll— But for me, Evvie would have died of thirst."

This was to Wade, and to Harvey, who came to join them.

"I doubt it," Harvey said. "She's a big girl now. Spreading your wing again, Bonny? Mother henning?"

"Not me," Bonita said. "Form a hollow square, boys. Women and children first. It's a wonderful party, Mother Landcraft." The last was louder. "And *Life* really came."

"Glad you think so," Margaret Landcraft said, with no evidence that she meant a word of it. She looked at Bonita as if she had not been looking at her before. "I do hope you don't catch cold," Mrs. Landcraft said. "It turns cool after the sun goes down, this time of year. In the country."

"You mustn't worry, dear," Bonita said, all concern. "I never do. Do I, Harv?"

"Never," Harvey Landcraft said. "She never does, mother." He was more firm about it than one is usually firm about so little. "Don't you think she's looking well?"

"Very," Mrs. Landcraft said. "I merely felt that perhaps she was not very warmly—"

"Yes," Harvey said. "We both understand. Can't I get you something?"

"Not now," Mrs. Landcraft said. "Food's ready." She

raised her voice. "Food when you want it," she said, generally. A number nodded and smiled and continued to drink. "Try to get them started, Wade," Mrs. Landcraft said. She was abrupt.

"Yes'm boss," Wade said. "Dinner's served, Evvie." But he had an almost full drink in his hand, and he sipped from it, and showed no immediate intention of doing more.

His mother looked at him and waited. She was not pleased; her tanned, ruddy face grew perceptibly more ruddy. She looked at her younger son intently, but of this Wade seemed unaware. Then she turned her intent, her insistent, gaze on Evelyn Merritt, and pointedly waited. An offer herself to "get them started" hesitated on Evelyn's lips, and she stopped it there. "Watch yourself, lady." So she merely smiled, pleasantly, pointedly unaware of stress.

Mrs. Landcraft continued to wait, and the waiting time passed slowly, grindingly. But finally she merely made a sound, which was not a word, and turned and went off among her guests. She strode off.

"They'd better snap into it," Bonita Landcraft said to no one in particular. "If they know what's good for them they—"

"O.K., Bonny," her husband said. "O.K. The point's made."

"Oh hell," Wade said. "I'll pass the word. Come along, Evvie?"

"The point's unmade," Bonita said.

But at that, Evelyn shook her head. She put a hand on Wade's arm, went beside him to pass the word.

"On the whole," Bonita said to her husband, "I guess she's right at that."

"You're very subtle," Harvey said. "Or something. You do rub her the wrong way, Bonny."

"I?" Bonny said. "More rubbed against than rubbing."

"She's all right," Harvey said. "Likes to have her own way. So do you, come down to it."

"Like to have my own man," Bonita said. "Not anybody's son. See what I mean, darling?"

She was told she was clear enough, that she made too much of it.

"What the hell?" Harvey said. "A couple of times a year." He smiled suddenly. "So you never catch cold, don't you?"

"Well, almost never," Bonita said. "And thanks for the vote of confidence."

"Probably," Harvey said, "you were standing with the light behind you. A matter of legs."

"So?" Bonny said, and the quick grin came again. It was, Harvey thought, a grin which ought to go with freckles. "Just because Angus have none to speak of?" She sobered. "The point is she hates me. She'll hate Evelyn when she and Wade are married. That's the point. It's not a funny point, darling."

"I wouldn't call it that," Harvey said. "Hate, I mean. Anyway, it's not you exactly."

"What, then?"

Harvey was silent a moment. Then he shrugged.

"Possibly," he said, "she thinks that if you weren't around—and Evvie wasn't—we could all settle down and concentrate. Here, I mean. On the Deep Meadow Herd. On getting a grand champion of all grand champions."

"Wade doesn't give a damn," Bonita said. "You're one of the best around in video. Doesn't she—?"

"No," Harvey said. "She doesn't. She never will. And—it's something we have to worry about a couple of times a year, isn't it?"

"Oftener than that. But, yes, I suppose so. I think I'd like—" She looked at the bar, now only desultorily in action. "No," she said. "I guess not. As you said, the point's made—whatever it was. Let's eat."

A line was forming, now, at one end of the buffet table. Evelyn and Wade were in it. They dropped back to join Harvey and Bonita at the end. The four filled plates, found a table at which four could sit. They had half finished when an ample woman in a print dress walked across the lawn toward them. She held a plate in one hand and an old-fashioned in the other. She had white hair in a coil, and a firm pink face and small blue eyes. She said, "Hello, folks. Room for one more?" There was great cheer in her voice.

"Hi, Florrie," Wade said. "Lots of room. Get you a chair." He was standing by then, as was Harvey. "Florrie Haskins," Wade said. He named the others. "Missis Haskins," Harvey repeated and the pink-cheeked woman said, "Miss, young man," and put her plate down. She retained her glass and took a deep drink from it. Wade came back with a chair. They sidled chairs together and made room.

"What's the matter with the big 'un?" Miss Florence Haskins asked, and, with some intentness, speared a piece of cold turkey.

"Prince?" Wade said. "The matter?"

"Peaked," Miss Haskins said. "Don't tell me, Wade. Off his feed?"

"Come off it, Florrie," Wade said, and grinned at her. "You're jealous."

"Sure I am," Miss Haskins said. "Good beef. Yours?" She chewed, contentedly.

"No," Wade said. "There's nothing the matter with Prince."

"Don't tell me," she said. "I just came from the barn. Look." She indicated her feet, in brown oxfords, fashioned for support. The oxfords were stained. "Went in his stall. Pushed him around. He's peaked."

"Listen," Bonita said. "This is Deep Meadow Prince you're talking about. A big *bull?* You pushed him around?"

Wade and Miss Haskins looked at her with surprise which seemed honest. Harvey widened his eyes, lifted his eyebrows. "City girl," he told them all. Bonny said, "No, really?"

"Prince is as gentle as a kitten," Wade said. "Children can push him around, Bonny. Children have."

"The milk of bovine kindness," Harvey said. He saw disbelief in his wife's brown eyes. "Really," he said. "Likes to have his ears scratched. Phlegmatic type."

"I suppose," Bonita said, "he likes to smell flowers?"

"Probably," Wade told her. "He's never said, but probably."

Bonita looked at Evelyn, who nodded. She looked at Florence Haskins.

"Sure," Florrie said. "Quiet as they come. Most of the doddies are."

"Look," Bonita said. "He's a bull. He must weigh—oh, tons."

"A ton and a bit," Wade said.

"And," Bonny said, "people push him around?"

Florence Haskins laughed at that. She said people pushed. "He doesn't give much," she admitted.

Bonita Landcraft studied four faces, with the air of one who suspects a point missed. She looked longest, most enquiringly, at Evelyn Merritt, and Evelyn smiled, and nodded quickly, reassuringly.

"All right," Bonny said. "It sounds funny to me." She considered. "Of course," she said, "I don't meet many bulls." She returned to her plate.

"He doesn't weigh over two thousand now," Florence Haskins said. "Or not by much. You can't tell me, Wade."

"Oh," Wade said. "That's what you meant. Yes, Alec's fined him down a bit. Vet said he needed it."

"Peaked, if you ask me," Florrie Haskins said. "Not what he was."

"You hope," Wade told her. "Florrie's the Rocking River Herd," he told the others. "Got a bull she claims is as good as Prince. Only—Prince won the big one. Right, Florrie?"

"With some of the judges you run into—" Florence Haskins said, and stopped. "All right, Wade," she said. "I'd get a new vet. Or a new—" Again she broke off. "It's your herd," she said. "Or Margaret's."

"Hers," Wade said. "And Ballard's good. You know that, Florrie."

"Sure," Florrie Haskins said. She speared the coiled pinkness of a shrimp and her plate was empty. She looked at her glass, and saw it empty too.

"Get you something?" Wade asked. She hesitated, shook her head. She waved a hand, unexpectedly small, in front of her considerable abdomen. "Got to remember," she said. She stood up, and the men stood. They were told to sit down. "Want to walk around a little," Miss Haskins said, and walked, carrying her glass. She walked toward the bar, and lights went on in a string above it.

"Saw her start," Wade said, amusement in his voice. "Quite an old girl, Florrie. Got quite a herd, too. Up in Dutchess. Bigger than ours, but no grand champion. Irks her a bit."

"Look," Harvey said, "there isn't anything wrong with the old boy, is there? He's where the money is, you know."

Wade looked across at him, smiling slightly, the smile not quite straight.

"I do know," he said. "No, he's all right, Harv. Trimmed down a bit, as I told Florrie. Perhaps a little more than—" He broke off. "The vet and Ballard know their business," he said. "Mother agrees with them, which settles it."

It was a few minutes before eight that the lights went on over the bar; that two of Mr. Pringle's waiters began moving from table to table, lighting candles in hurricane chimneys. (But the evening was so still that unprotected flames would hardly have flickered. Nor had the temperature fallen appreciably as the shadows lengthened.) Beyond the hills the sky had burned, then smouldered. People sat at tables still, and smoked and drank; they walked in the dusk, and cigarettes formed little groups, like congregated fireflies. The groups formed, dissolved, reconstituted. The conversation was of cattle, of sales of the previous spring and those set for late winter; of shows past and still to come.

It was afterward difficult to establish the whereabouts of anyone between eight or thereabouts and eleven forty-five. Those who were asked had answers ready enough, but the answers were vague. Wade Landcraft and Alec Ballard, the farm manager, had "circulated." Harvey had, with another drink, talked for some time with a man he had run into, and not quite clearly got the name of, and had talked about sports cars. Arnold Thayer had visited the barns, with two other breeders, and they had left the barns at a quarter of ten. They agreed about that; but afterward they had separated. Thayer had sat for a time, for long enough to smoke a cigar, in a chair at one end of the terrace and then, since he was staying overnight at the Landcrafts', had gone up to his room. He had gone up, he thought, at a few minutes after eleven.

Bonita Landcraft and Evelyn could confirm part of that —could confirm, at any rate, that someone had sat in a terrace chair and smoked alone. But as to time, they could tell little. And Bonita, at a time also not definite but considerably before eleven forty-five, had got up from the chair in which she had been sitting, talking to Evelyn beside her, and remarked that when a girl had to go she had to go. Bonita had thereupon gone. Evelyn, relaxed, with a forgotten drink, had sat on, thinking of Wade. She had been almost dozing at eleven forty.

The time became important because, at eleven forty-five, Deep Meadow Prince bellowed furiously from his box stall in the nearest barn—bellowed and kept on bellowing. After a time, lesser bulls in the other barns bellowed too. They made a great noise in the soft night.

It was rather theatrical that, at almost the same time, thunder began to roll behind the hills which lay protectingly around Deep Meadow Farm.

II

CAPTAIN M. L. HEIMRICH of the New York State Police read the *New York Times,* ate a sandwich and drank thick black coffee in the barracks of Troop K in Hawthorne. The news in the *Times* was, as usual, depressing; the situation of mankind continued to deteriorate. Captain Heimrich was mildly cheered by the thought that, when he finished lunch, he would start on a brief leave, which he could use. The case he had just completed had been tedious—a hit and run with complications, involving people unrelievedly dull, hackneyed homicide and motives as obvious as methods. It had, nevertheless, taken time and much plodding; Heimrich felt as if, for two weeks and more, he had been slogging along a featureless road, ankle-deep in dust. He proposed now to lie somewhere on sand, now and then to dunk himself in ocean.

Captain Heimrich wore glasses as he read the *Times.* He was a broad man and a solid one. His face appeared, now as he read and ate, to be a carving from some hard and darkened wood. He finished his coffee, neatly rearranged the *Times* and then dropped it into a waste-paper basket. He folded the paper in which his sandwich had been wrapped and dropped the neat square in the basket with the *Times*.

A uniformed trooper, young, properly wedge-shaped, walked to the desk Heimrich occupied and stood in front of it, his stance military. He said, "Sir."

"Yes?" Heimrich said.

"The sergeant said I should take it up with you, captain," the trooper said. "He says there's nothing to it, but take it up with you if I want to. My name's Crowley, captain. Brewster sub-station. About this thing at the Landcraft place, sir."

Heimrich merely shook his head.

"It was in the papers," Crowley said. "Nothing much. I've got it here some place. On page ten of the *Times*." He reached toward his hip pocket. Heimrich reached into the waste-paper basket and retrieved the *Times*. He turned to page ten. "There," Crowley said, and pointed. Heimrich read:

BULL TRAMPLES BREEDER

Brewster Woman Hurt Fatally
by Enraged Angus

He read on. The dateline was Brewster, New York. He read:

"Mrs. Margaret Landcraft, widely known breeder of Aberdeen Angus cattle and owner of Deep Meadow Farm three miles north of this Putnam County village, was fatally injured late tonight when a prize bull, supposedly gentle, trampled her in its stall in one of the farm barns.

"The accident occurred during a buffet supper Mrs. Landcraft was giving prior to the annual sale at Deep Meadow Farm, which was to have been held tomorrow. More than a hundred persons, including Mrs. Landcraft's two sons, were within sight of the barn in which the accident occurred. Several, including the sons, Harvey and Wade Landcraft, ran to the scene when they heard the bull bellowing violently, but arrived only to find Mrs. Landcraft dead in the animal's stall.

"The animal was generally considered harmless, according to Wade Landcraft, who assisted his mother in operation of the farm, and Alec Ballard, the farm manager. What caused it to turn on its owner is unknown."

Heimrich finished reading and took off his glasses. He looked at Trooper Crowley.

"Regrettable, naturally," Heimrich said. "But we can't arrest the bull, can we?"

The younger man flushed slightly. "No sir," he said. "The sergeant mentioned that, captain."

"I'm sure he did." Heimrich closed his eyes momentarily. He opened them. "Go ahead, Crowley."

"I know the bull," Crowley said. "Went around with Dad once to look at him. Wanted to see a cow worth eighty thousand dollars."

"Um-m," Heimrich said. "That much?"

"More, probably," Crowley said. "It's insured for that much. I understand it's as high as you can go. The Deep Meadow Angus are famous, captain."

Heimrich waited.

"He's a damn big animal, captain," Crowley said. "Weighs a ton anyway—more, probably. Got very short legs and no horns. Maybe you know that, sir?"

Heimrich shook his head.

"Black Angus are beef animals," Crowley said. "My father runs a dairy farm, but he's interested in Angus. Only —you've got to have a kind of money we haven't got."

Heimrich waited.

"Dad sells hay to Deep Meadow sometimes," Crowley said. "I went there with him once, and he showed me this bull. Dad went into his stall, pushed him and said, 'Move over, Prince,' and Prince just moved over. Dad said to come on in and look him over and I said, 'Not me.' Dad laughed and said he knew kittens that were more dangerous, that Prince wouldn't hurt a fly—or, he guessed, anything but a fly. Then when Dad heard about his being supposed to have trampled Mrs. Landcraft—well, he said he didn't think it was possible." Crowley paused. "Dad knows animals, captain."

Heimrich tapped the newspaper. "The bull bellowed," he said. "They found Mrs. Landcraft in the stall. Somewhat—battered, I gather."

"He'd—well, it looked as if he'd walked on her, captain. She was—all crushed. Broken. She was a big woman. Big and strong. And—she knew animals too. Prince especially."

"I don't know animals," Heimrich said. "It seems to me I've heard bulls are not to be trusted. That they'll be gentle one minute and berserk the next."

Crowley nodded. "That's what they say."

"But?"

"Well," Crowley said, and hesitated. "I suppose that was

it. Only—well, Dad knows a lot about cattle, captain. If he says Prince is gentle—well—"

"Apparently he killed this woman."

Crowley nodded.

"The doctor's satisfied?"

Crowley nodded again.

"The bull killed her," he said. "I guess there's no doubt about that. I suppose it's just the way it looks. All right, sir. I'll—"

But Captain Heimrich had closed his eyes. He made a slight movement of one hand, and Crowley waited. Heimrich opened his eyes.

"I suppose somebody could stir up the most gentle animal," he said. "Goad him. That's what your father thinks?"

"Yes," Crowley said. "That is—he's got no way of knowing."

"The county people are satisfied, I take it?"

"Yes sir. Seem to be, anyway."

"Yes," Heimrich said. "Aside from your father's conviction the bull's gentle, is there something else, Crowley? You know these people, naturally. You know what I mean."

"Well," Crowley said, "I can't say I know them, captain. Just met them. Somebody banged up their mailbox—went along for a couple of miles banging up all the mailboxes. You know how it is. I met Mrs. Landcraft then. She was pretty sore."

"Yes," Heimrich said. "You find out who did it, Crowley?"

Crowley shook his head.

"No," Heimrich said. "I didn't suppose you had. You

know the sons?" He checked with the *Times*. "Wade and Harvey? They live there?"

Wade did; Harvey lived in New York. Crowley thought that Harvey—the elder of the two—visited the farm only occasionally. "Got a wife doesn't like the country much, from what I hear," Crowley said. "Show girl they say she is. On television."

Heimrich smiled faintly, for the most part inwardly. Things got around in the country. A good trooper absorbed, hardly knowing he did so. Crowley was on his way, apparently, to becoming a good trooper. Heimrich nodded.

"Wade's planning to marry the Merritt girl," Crowley said. "Nice people, the Merritts. Been in the county a long time. Almost as long as the Wades."

"Wades?"

"Mrs. Landcraft was a Wade."

The bull was not alone in having pedigree, Heimrich thought, and did not say. Instead, he said he gathered there was no older male Landcraft. Mrs. Landcraft had been a widow? Or divorced?

She had been a widow; the widow of John Hamilton Landcraft, and at the name Heimrich nodded. It was little more than a name to him, but it was to some degree a name to almost everyone. Landcraft had been a corporation lawyer of renown and, presumably, of high fees. Crowley told what he knew, starting with that.

John—John Hamilton—Landcraft had bought Deep Meadow Farm some forty years before and taken up the breeding of Aberdeen Angus, more or less as a hobby. He must have had a good deal of money; as a hobby the breeding of pedigreed cattle can come high. Shortly after buying the farm, he had married Margaret Wade, the daughter of a neighbor, and then in her early twenties. Landcraft himself must have been forty.

"This was all before my time," Crowley said. "But you pick things up. You know how it is, sir."

Heimrich nodded to that.

Landcraft and his wife had lived on the farm, expanding the herd slowly, for some twenty-five years. A great deal of money had gone into the farm, but Landcraft apparently was making plenty. They had produced, in addition to prize cattle, two sons. Then, in his late sixties, when Mrs. Landcraft was around fifty, Landcraft had died. That would be—"oh, about a dozen years ago. I was a kid and I remember watching the funeral. Biggest one we'd ever had around there."

Mrs. Landcraft had continued to run the farm. Wade had gone to Cornell, taking the agricultural course. Harvey, the elder, had gone to Dartmouth.

"Still plenty of money," Heimrich said.

Crowley hesitated. He said, then, that he supposed so. "At a guess," he said, "it's mostly tied up in the place. You don't get cattle like that for peanuts. The whole shebang costs plenty to run. They've got farm trucks and a couple of station wagons but Mrs. Landcraft drove around mostly in a 1950 Plymouth. Good car and all that but—well, most of the people around there—people with big places—go in for Cadillacs. You get the picture, sir?"

Heimrich closed his eyes. This time he did not immediately reopen them, and when he spoke it was not in direct answer to Crowley's question, which at the moment was, in any case, unanswerable.

"When you come down to it," he said, "all you've got's a hunch. That's it, isn't it?"

The good-looking young man flushed under his tan. He said, "O.K., sir. Sorry I took your time," and started to stand up. Heimrich opened his eyes, then.

"Now Crowley," he said. "Sit down. What's wrong with having a hunch?"

Crowley sat down, but he shook his head.

"A good deal of the job's in having hunches," Heimrich said. "Get a hunch, check up on hunch. You see some men in a car and something doesn't look right. Just a hunch. So you check up. Most of the time, everything is right, naturally. Sometimes it isn't. You work that way?"

"Oh," Crowley said, "sure."

"Sure," Heimrich repeated. "So do I. You've got a hunch there's something wrong with this Landcraft setup. The bull's too gentle. But there's something more. What is it?"

Crowley shook his head again.

"Now trooper," Heimrich said. "Think."

Crowley appeared to. He spoke hesitantly.

"Nearly as I can say it," he said, "it's the wrong thing to have happened to her—the wrong kind of thing. You—well, you just can't figure her having an accident."

Heimrich waited.

"She was a big woman," Crowley said. "Bigger than most men. And—she seemed to sort of run things, if you know what I mean. Be in charge of them. You figure—oh, with some people a car's going to get away from them, or a ladder's going to break, or a knife slip. Some people—" He stopped. He shrugged. He looked at Heimrich, and Heimrich, his eyes wide open now, nodded. "Hell," Crowley said, "you just wouldn't figure an accident would have the nerve to happen to Mrs. Landcraft."

Heimrich nodded again. But he said, "Of course, a bull isn't exactly an accident, in that sense. But I see what you mean. She sounds like a forceful woman."

"You can say that again."

Heimrich closed his eyes, in passive rejection of a locution he found trying.

"Difficult to live with, probably," he said.

"About that, I don't know, sir," Trooper Crowley said. "Like I said, I only met her a couple of times. But maybe —well, they say she did have run-ins with some of the people around here. Nothing serious. You know the sort of thing. Nothing anybody would get really—well, sore about. Anyhow, not sore enough to—" He stopped.

"Stir up the animals," Heimrich said. "In this case, literally. But—you've a hunch someone did. Your father has. You'd—what? Been expecting something?"

"If I was, I didn't know it," the trooper said. "Maybe. But—"

"But not this," Heimrich said. "Not an accident in a bull pen." He paused. "I can't recall," he said, "ever having heard of murder by bull. Rather an interesting notion. Not that there's anything to go on, naturally. The sheriff's satisfied, you say? The D. A.?"

"Yes," Crowley said.

"But," Heimrich said, "you had to have a hunch. I'd have started a few days' leave"—he looked at his watch—"half an hour ago. Sergeant Forniss, who works with me, has already started his." He looked at Crowley, with slight reproach.

Crowley started to say he was sorry, but Heimrich shook his head.

"It's all right," he said. "I'd rather like to see this bull that's so damn gentle."

He got up. He was a very solid man.

"You may as well come along with me, Crowley," he said. "Maybe you'll have another hunch."

III

THEY HAD BEEN polite at Carmel, the county seat. The district attorney had been polite; the medical examiner had been polite. There had been hardly anything in the attitude of either, or of the detectives of the district attorney's office, to indicate a suspicion that Captain M. L. Heimrich, of the criminal identification division of the New York State Police, had taken leave of his senses. If he was not satisfied with the obvious facts, the fullest cooperation of everyone would, naturally, be offered—was offered, then and there. But, the facts were obvious.

"She went into the stall—it's really a pen—with this big bull," the district attorney explained, and he was patient. "The bull was loose in the stall. You know what bulls are, captain. Anybody's crazy who trusts a bull."

This particular bull, Heimrich pointed out, mildly, was supposed to be gentle. He didn't, he added, know much about bulls. He could not remember that, in his experience, bulls had previously come up.

"Everybody knows you can't trust a bull," the district attorney said. "Maybe they act gentle, sure. Maybe they're gentle for a long time. Then they turn and gore you. While back, a farmer around here was damn near killed by a bull he'd raised from a calf. It used to follow him around. Hell, it used to try to follow him into the house and when it couldn't it'd stand outside and cry. That's what they say, anyhow. So, one day when the bull was three, four years old, it turned on the man and knocked him down and gored him. Put him in the hospital for months." He regarded Heimrich; he spoke with finality. "That's the way bulls are, captain," he said. "You can't trust them."

Heimrich nodded. He'd heard that, naturally. No doubt it was true. Was Mrs. Landcraft gored?

"Well," the district attorney said, "no, she wasn't. She was just sort of—well, crushed. You know why that was, captain? The bull hasn't got any horns. That's the only reason. He did all right without them."

"You raise cattle yourself?" Heimrich asked, and was looked at with astonishment.

"Good God no," the district attorney said. "What's that got to do with it?"

Heimrich agreed that it had probably nothing to do with anything.

"Young Crowley's just proving what a smart cop he is," the district attorney said. "But it's up to you, captain. As I said, we'll cooperate." He paused. "Fully," he said. "Just bring us something." He smiled, faintly, at his own words. Heimrich went to talk to the doctor who had examined what remained of Mrs. Margaret Landcraft, recently so resolute.

"Crushed," the doctor said, succinctly. "A ton of bull leaned on her. Knocked her down and trampled her. From the looks, he might have rolled on her. She might as well have been pushed against a brick wall by a truck."

"The bull was supposed to be gentle," Heimrich said.

"I heard that story," the doctor said. "Also, I saw what he did to the woman. Maybe he had been and—well, went bad. That happens, you know. Stallions. Bulls. As a matter of fact, even tomcats. Friend of mine had a cat for years. Nice, friendly cat. All at once, it turned savage and clawed my friend up. Had to have it killed. Just as they will this bull, probably. Remember, when they used to use work cattle, they turned them into oxen."

Probably he was right. Males did, sometimes, grow more deadly as they grew older. Did the doctor know whether this bull had been getting along in years?

The doctor did not. All he knew about the bull was that he was black, and low-slung, and apparently had got his owner in a corner and killed her. That was what he had been told, anyway. The body had been removed from the stall when he saw it. He understood that somebody—he thought a photographer from some magazine or other—had taken a picture before the body was removed. Although what he planned to do with it, the doctor couldn't guess. It wouldn't have been pretty.

"No," Heimrich said. "You didn't find anything that was out of line? No injuries the bull might not have caused?"

"She wasn't shot, or stabbed or poisoned," the doctor said. "I take it that's what you have in mind?"

"Now doctor," Heimrich said, and closed his eyes briefly. "I haven't anything in mind. I'm told the bull was gentle. Always had been. Crowley's father knows cattle, the boy tells me."

"Listen," the doctor said, "there was a man around here —a man who knew cattle as well as Crowley does—who practically brought a bull calf up by hand. Then one day—"

"Yes," Heimrich said. "I heard. You didn't notice anything out of the way?"

"She was dead," the doctor said. "She was alive when the bull started on her. She died, primarily any way, of a crushed chest. The bull killed her."

"Yes," Heimrich said. "Well."

He stood up.

"What probably happened," the doctor said, "was that she started to do something to the bull and he turned on her. Maybe he had a scratch, and she was putting disinfectant of some kind on it. Something with carbolic in it, probably. It stung and—well, the bull got mad."

"Hm-m," Heimrich said. "Was there a scratch on the bull?"

"My god, captain," the doctor said. "You think I examined the bull, too?"

"Now doctor," Heimrich said. "No. I just wondered what made you think of that—that she was treating the bull."

For a moment, the physician looked slightly puzzled. Then he shook his head, said he didn't know. Then he smiled, rather as the district attorney had.

"You seemed to want an explanation," he said. "That just came into my head. I don't know why. Probably there's nothing to it. Probably the bull just turned savage."

"Yes," Heimrich said, "no doubt that's all there is to it."

He thanked the physician; was promised any cooperation possible; thanked him again. He joined Trooper Crowley in the police car parked in front of the county court house. He told Crowley that everybody believed the bull had turned savage.

"Dad says he was a gentle bull," Crowley told him. "But —I suppose they're right, captain. You want to go back to Hawthorne?"

"Now Crowley," Heimrich had said. "We haven't had a look at this bull yet, have we?"

They had driven toward Brewster on U.S. 6, but had turned off while still several miles north of the town and had followed a secondary road—"Old Road"—for perhaps a mile before they came to a sign which read: "Deep Meadow Farm" and which had, beneath the lettering, the pictured face of a black bull. They went up a climbing drive, then, and stopped in front of a rambling white house. As Crowley parked the car, a man came from behind the house and stopped and stood looking at them, waiting. The man was tall, heavy. His florid face was without particular expression.

"Ballard," Crowley said. "Farm manager." Then, raising his voice, he said, "Back again, Mr. Ballard."

Ballard moved a few steps toward them.

"Didn't expect you," he said. He looked at Heimrich. "Captain Heimrich," Crowley said. Ballard took another step toward them. He said, "Captain, huh? Something come up?" Ballard asked.

"Come up?" Heimrich repeated. "No, not that I know of. Just a formality, Mr.—Ballard, is it?"

"Ballard," the big man agreed. "What's the formality?"

"Now Mr. Ballard," Heimrich said. "We have to keep the record straight, naturally. Probably won't have to bother you again. Just look over the scene of the accident, you know. Check up on a few things."

Ballard appeared to be puzzled. There was no reason, Heimrich thought, why he shouldn't be. It sounded thin. It was thin. The whole business was thin as glass, and less substantial. Ballard said, "O.K. What things?"

"Well," Heimrich said, "I'd like a look at the stall. And the bull. Unless he's been destroyed?"

Ballard's expression, then, was one of more than puzzlement. It was one of open and complete astonishment.

"Destroyed?" he said. "Prince? The *champ*? Are you crazy, mister?"

"Apparently," Heimrich said. "I don't know much about cattle, Mr. Ballard. It occurred to me that, if the animal's turned savage, it might be necessary to destroy him. Apparently I was—"

"Kill Prince?" Ballard said. "Mister, he's the grand champion." He looked at Heimrich; Heimrich felt himself inadequate to respond appropriately to this information. "The *International* Grand Champion," Ballard said, and spoke in capital letters. "That means he's the best Angus bull in the world. The—" Words appeared to fail him. He looked a man not given to emotion, but at the enormity of what had been suggested he spread large hands in a gesture of hopelessness. He looked toward the sky, as if seeking inspiration, and there, it appeared, he found it. "Deep Meadow Prince Twelfth, mister," he said, "is worth a quarter of a million dollars. The old girl—I mean, Mrs. Landcraft—wouldn't have sold him for that, and she'd have been a fool to. Where would she have been?"

"Now Mr. Ballard," Heimrich said. "I don't know. You mean—literally a quarter of a million?"

"Maybe more," Ballard said. "How can you tell? Nobody ever sells an international grand champion." He paused. "One was sold once," he said. "Brought two hundred thousand. That was several years ago and the Blacks have been coming along since." He looked at Heimrich again, and then he shook his head. "You don't know much about cattle, do you, mister?"

"No," Heimrich said. "I just said that, Mr. Ballard. I know very little about cattle of any kind."

"You don't know *anything* about Angus, mister?" His voice pleaded.

"Now Mr. Ballard," Heimrich said. "Something, yes. This bull you're talking about killed Mrs. Landcraft."

Looking at Ballard, Heimrich was struck by an odd idea—that Ballard had, during the past few moments, entirely forgotten the unfortunate incident of which he was now reminded.

Ballard's expression, which had been one of intense concentration on the subject at hand, altered. Ballard sighed, and shook his head. He said it was a terrible thing.

"Can't understand it," he said. "I'd have sworn she knew bulls. Then—she goes and does something and this happens."

"You think she did something to the bull? Something he—objected to?"

"Sure," Ballard said. "Must have been that. Usually, he'll do what you tell him. Do anything I tell him, anyway."

"Gentle, usually?" Heimrich said, but now Ballard hesitated for a moment.

"Sure," he said, after that moment. "Of course, I don't say you can trust Prince completely, or any bull. But, as bulls go—" He ended with a shrug. He added, "Sure, I'd call him gentle." He paused again. "You want to see him?" he asked. "See where it happened?"

"Yes," Heimrich said. "I'd like to, Mr. Ballard," and was told to come on, then. Ballard turned away and walked along a road which led around the house, and Heimrich and Trooper Crowley walked after him. Ballard took long strides.

When they came out beyond the house, he stopped for a moment, and Heimrich stopped too, and looked at the great sweep of green, cupped in green hills; looked at the barns, lower down the slope. To the left of the barns, a little more distant from the house than the barns, several men were working. They were taking down a large tent.

"Sale tent," Ballard said, without being asked. "If this hadn't happened, there'd be a couple of hundred people here—breeders from all over. We were having the sale today. Had to call it off, of course. Tough break. Come along."

They went along, down a road to the first of the barns—a long white building, with a hay loft above, open at either end. Ballard led them in—led them to unexpected coolness, to the faint hum of electric fans, to the not unpleasant odor of cattle.

To their left, as they stood just inside the double, opened doors, there were stalls against the wall—more accurately, Heimrich thought, they were pens, since only heavy wooden fencing, less than shoulder high, separated them from the wide central passage which ran the length of the building. In the first of these pens, three medium-sized black cattle seemed to be kneeling in deep straw. They regarded the visitors with mild curiosity, through mild eyes. On the other side there was a row of vari-colored cattle, their backs to the audience, their necks confined between vertical, parallel bars of metal.

"Some of the bull calves," Ballard said, pointing to the apparently kneeling animals. "The nurses." He pointed to the tan cows, the black and white cows, full-uddered and lazily tail-switching. "Keep the calves on milk as long as we can and when their mothers don't have enough these" —he again indicated the bovine rumps on his right—"adopt them. Jersey and Guernseys for the bulls, Holsteins for the heifers, of course."

"Oh," Heimrich said. "Of course."

"Come along, then," Ballard said, and walked on clean cement, dusted with white powder. They walked past a second pen on the left, in which there were four more black cattle, also apparently on their knees.

"Some of the heifers," Ballard said. "That one's Bessie." He pointed. "She's a real baby doll," he said. "Come on."

They went on. Two thirds down the long barn, Ballard stopped abruptly. Here there was a much larger pen—twenty feet by fifteen or sixteen, Heimrich estimated. In the most distant corner a small cat, a blotched tabby, crouched motionless, staring at the straw, in the immemorial stance of a cat anticipating mouse. Ballard put his elbows on the top rail of the barricade and Heimrich and Crowley joined him.

"Well," Ballard said, "there's the champ."

They looked—looked down on a murderer. Deep Meadow Prince Twelfth turned his heavy head slightly, and looked up at them. He had large round eyes, which appeared to be black or a very deep purple, just perceptibly rimmed with brown. He had a knob of bone in the middle of his forehead, and no horns. Ears jutted enterprisingly from either side of the massive head. And the bull's expression was one of utter benignity.

The little cat leaped at moving straw, in a flash of sudden violence. The bull turned and looked at her, and looked away again, and again at the men. The cat came out with a mouse, which had one squeal left. The cat carried her mouse toward them, and underneath the great barrel of the bull, and between bars of the fence, and toward one of the doors. As she passed under the bull, she brushed one of his black legs. Prince ignored this; now he ignored the men, and turned to nibble hay. He nibbled delicately.

"Well, mister," Ballard said, "you're looking at what I'd call the greatest bull in the world."

Heimrich looked—looked down the great body, realized that this bull was not kneeling, although his belly almost grazed the straw in which he stood. The bull had no legs to speak of. Compared to him, the Jerseys and Guernseys they had passed earlier were built like deer. It occurred to Heimrich, unexpectedly, that the broad, perfectly level back of the black bull was precisely at a convenient patting height. And, as he continued to look at the black bull—from massive head, which still did not seem heavy, along short neck, past great smooth shoulders and tremendous body, to rounded rump, to tasseled tail which brushed the straw—it occurred to Heimrich that he was looking at something very like perfection.

He did not then try consciously to explain this feeling to himself. Afterward, when it seemed desirable to find out what he could about Aberdeen Angus and he read what such a bull should be, more specific knowledge rather confused than brightened his first impression of Deep Meadow Prince. In those first minutes, Heimrich knew without deciding, he looked as closely as he was ever likely to look on perfect symmetry.

He was conscious, of course, of mass, and of great strength. But nowhere did strength bulge, nowhere was there any awkwardness. Broad-backed as the bull was, short-legged as he was, there was no suggestion of—Heimrich sought a word—"sluggishness" in the whole design. Perhaps, Heimrich decided, the simplest explanation of the sense of satisfaction one derived from looking at Deep Meadow Prince was that the animal, for what had been planned, was precisely right. Beyond any living thing Heimrich could remember seeing, this bull was of one piece.

Having reached that conclusion—while a quarter of million dollars' worth of bull continued abstractedly to nibble hay—Heimrich heard Ballard say, in tones of deep satisfaction, "Now there, mister, is a real soggy bull. A *deep* soggy bull."

Captain Heimrich detached his attention from Deep Meadow Prince and looked at Ballard in astonishment. He closed his eyes, and took a deep breath. He opened his eyes.

"Soggy?" he repeated, and his voice remained mild. It remained so by an effort. He looked again at Prince—at a ton or so of as solid material as he had seen in animal form. "That's soggy?" Captain Heimrich said.

Ballard laughed, shortly. He said it was a term.

"Yes," Heimrich said. "I supposed that, naturally." Nevertheless, he shook his head.

"Show you," Ballard said, and raised the latch which—not securely enough, Heimrich found himself abruptly thinking—held closed a gate in the barrier. Ballard entered the pen with Prince. Heimrich looked at Trooper Crowley, and detected—or suspected—a faint look of amusement in the young man's eyes. That would not do, of course. Heimrich entered the stall after Ballard. Ballard thumped the big bull on the hip, and the bull moved slightly, providing additional room. He also turned his large head and regarded Ballard with very mild interest.

"Feel him," Ballard said, and Heimrich felt. The smooth black hair was surprisingly soft to the touch. "Push down," Ballard said. Heimrich looked briefly into Prince's large round eyes, and pushed. Unexpectedly, the bull's flesh gave—gave resistingly, softly. It was as if Heimrich pressed a yielding, yet resilient, rubber mattress. "See?" Ballard said. "That's what we call soggy. Don't want them tight, of course."

Mr. Ballard was enjoying all this, Heimrich realized. Ballard did not need urging and Heimrich, who was interested—but did not see where he was getting, except that the bull now, at any rate, seemed gentle enough—waited.

"You see, mister," Ballard said, "this is a beef animal. That's what the blacks are, beef cattle. See—roasts." He patted the great side of the animal. "Steaks." He patted further aft. "Rump steaks, roasts." He patted suitably.

Deep Meadow Prince continued to regard the two men. He did not seem offended. Heimrich trusted he would not be.

"When they're soggy," Ballard said, "it shows they'll fatten smoothly. Room to grow, in a way. See what I mean?"

"Yes," Heimrich said.

"Make prize carcasses," Ballard said. "Best beef there is, Angus." He patted the big bull again, with what appeared to be affection. And the great animal, whose comprehension of English seemed a little dull, turned his head further toward the men, so that Ballard could reach the broad forehead, with the bony protuberance at the top, under the black-haired hide. "That's the poll," Ballard said, patting it. Then he more or less leaned on the bull. This seemed to please Prince, moderately.

"Perfect poll," Ballard said. "Perfect style all the way back. Look at that tail."

Heimrich looked at the tail.

"No need to give him a switch," Ballard said. "You can see that, mister."

Heimrich did what was evidently expected. He repeated the word, "Switch?"

"Doddies are expected to have tails like that," Ballard said. "Typy—whole animal wants to be typy. Some pretty good animals don't have the right kind of tails. So, I've known breeders would work a switch in at the end to fix the tail up. When they were showing, that is. Only trouble is, any judge knows his business gives the tail a yank. Seen them come right off in the judge's hand." He moved to the rear of Prince, took the long tail in his hand and yanked, with no especial gentleness. "Can't pull that one off," he said. Prince turned his head further and looked at Ballard. Prince appeared only mildly interested.

"O.K.," Ballard said. "There's your bull. What else you want to know?"

"This is where it happened," Heimrich said. "Where, precisely, Mr. Ballard?"

Ballard pointed to a corner of the stall, where heavy fence met wall.

"Got her over there," he said. "Knocked her down—maybe just—well, rammed her—and killed her standing. Trampled her." He looked at the straw in the corner. "Didn't bleed much," he said.

It was the same corner in which the little cat had caught her mouse. Some hours ago, the crushed body of a woman had lain there. The soft-eyed great creature—at whom, Heimrich suddenly realized—neither of them was now bothering to look, had killed there.

"Never know what she did," Ballard said. "What got him started. Nothing to show she hurt him." He turned back to the bull, and absently patted its forehead. "About all I can tell you," Ballard said. "What you wanted?"

"Now Mr. Ballard," Heimrich said. "I don't know. It is—well, puzzling, isn't it? He appears to be a very mild creature." Heimrich looked at him. "For his size," he added. "You don't keep him tethered, even. No ring in his nose."

"Not for the champ," Ballard said, and banged the big animal's hip. "Wouldn't like that, would you, champ? Trained to halter, of course. Shows well. Got style."

"When you show them," Heimrich said, "what do you do?"

"Do?" Ballard repeated. "Oh, lead them into the ring. Get them to put their heads up. They're all fitted, of course. We break the hair on the thighs and neck"—he indicated—"and curl it. Use a coat bloom, of course." He looked at Heimrich. "Hair oil," he explained. "First we've gone over the animal with a vacuum cleaner. Bush the tail out nice. Get them all dressed up for the party. Get them out in the ring and pose them—got to be trained to pose, of course, the doddies do. Some breeders figure the training is about as important as anything else—that the top animals at a big show don't differ too much, over all, and that the best trained ones win. At the International, this time, there were some pretty good bulls, but they were all trained. The champ here was tops in that, too."

He leaned on the bull, and waited.

"They don't mind all this?" Heimrich asked.

"Rather like it," Ballard said. "Most of them, anyhow. Course, if you get a mean one—but who wants a mean one? Want them nice and easy-going like the champ here and—"

He stopped, abruptly, with that. He looked at Heimrich.

"Yes," Heimrich said. "That's the trouble, isn't it? A good-tempered animal, used to people, to being shown, trained to the halter. He has been shown a lot, I suppose?"

"Well," Ballard said, "sure. Last year. Up to the International at Chicago. The circuit in the east, through the Eastern National at Timonium. That's in Maryland; it's tops for the east. Like the American Royal at K. C. is pretty much tops for the west. When he went grand champion at Timonium, we took him on to Chicago, and he went international grand champ."

"He'll be shown again?"

"Nope, he's had it. Once a two year old goes international grand champion, he can't compete again. This fellow might win for years if we could show him. Got to give the others a chance. Win again with one of his get, maybe."

"So now he's—" Heimrich did not finish.

"Herd bull," Ballard said. "Herd sire. Breed him a couple of times a week. Artificially, as we do it. Say he lives to be ten—he's three, now. Sire a million dollars' worth of animals, with any luck. See why nobody wants to sell him? And you talked about destroying him!"

He had been naïve, Heimrich realized.

"Up to now," he said, "I take it he's never seemed mean. It would be difficult to show a really mean bull, probably."

"Sure," Ballard said. "Nope—always been gentle as—well, as a heifer calf. Up to now." He looked at the bull. "What the hell happened to you?" he asked the animal, and Prince turned his head away and nibbled hay.

"This characteristic you call 'sogginess,'" Heimrich said. "I gather he passes it along."

"Sure," Ballard said. "That's the whole point, captain. You start with him—perfect type of the best beef animal in the world. His get—bulls and heifers—inherit his characteristics. That's the theory, anyway, and with breeders who know their business it mostly works out. Oh—now and then we get one that doesn't look like much, and maybe we steer him and fill a deep freeze. But that's incidental. The whole business is planned to end up with a lot of steers with characteristics like these"—he patted Prince—

"big, well-sprung ribs, smooth rumps, no waste to speak of in the neck or legs—just a hell of a lot of beef on the hoof. Out on a ranch in the west, maybe. Not pure breds, mostly. Blacks bred out of other stock, for the most part. But turning up the best meat. No horn bruises, for one thing. Doddies breed horns right off almost anything, so—"

He was, evidently, off again. But now Heimrich stopped him.

"Characteristics," he said. "They get passed along pretty consistently. And—bad disposition would too, Mr. Ballard? Meanness?"

That stopped Ballard. It stopped him abruptly. He looked steadily at Heimrich for some seconds.

"Might," he said. "A lot of people would figure it would, captain."

Heimrich nodded his head. He said, "Well—"

"Seen what you want to?" Ballard asked, and when Heimrich nodded, led the way out of the stall, into the central passage of the long barn.

"All you want to know?" Ballard asked, latching the gate. The bull moved to the fence and poked a black nose partly between two rails. "Wants to be petted," Ballard said, and rubbed the black nose.

"What happens now?" Heimrich asked. "To the herd, I mean?"

"Wouldn't know," Ballard said. "Have to ask the boys. The old girl's sons. Me, I wouldn't want to guess."

IV

THE PICTURE WOULD not leave Evelyn Merritt's mind—the first ugly picture of a woman broken, with a very little blood trickling from a corner of the mouth. Margaret Landcraft had been dead by then, but then they had not yet known it. Wade had cried, "Mother, you all right?" to dead ears, and Deep Meadow Prince had lifted his great head to bellow, and from the other bull in the barn, and from the bulls in the barn beyond, there came the same angry sound. But it had not seemed possible that Margaret Landcraft was dead. Only when they touched her, after Alec Ballard had slapped the big bull back—and how grotesque that it had taken no more than that!—had it been impossible to doubt.

Evelyn Merritt answered the telephone in the office in the Landcraft house. She said, "Yes, it is. We tried to reach everybody" and listened and said, "Yes, a dreadful thing" and, after listening again, said, "Thank you. I'll tell them" and replaced the receiver. It seemed, now in mid-afternoon, that she had been answering the telephone, or dialing Western Union on it, for all of the fifteen or so hours since the bull had first bellowed.

That was not strictly true; there had been, in the middle of the night, a little lull, and during it she had slept for a few hours, uncomfortably dreaming. She had wakened with her mind exhausted. She had been numb while she breakfasted, in a room into which sun poured, with Bonita Landcraft, who was pale that morning, although her lips were bright. But after that there had been so much to do that the numbness could not last.

They had done what they could the night before, with the State Police still there; with the photographers from *Life*, attending a party not anticipated, busy with cameras. Nobody had tried to stop the photographers, not even the police. The flashing of bulbs had become part of a turmoil so complete that no aspect of it could be separated out, dealt with. Most of the turmoil had had to do—and still had to do, for that matter—with the sale.

The decision to call it off had been made quickly. But, looking back on it now, sitting in front of the telephone, her hands on the desk idle, it seemed a little odd that it had had to be made at all. Margaret Landcraft was dead. That her sale could go on without her—setting aside all thought of propriety—was inconceivable. Wade had said that at once, but Harvey had hesitated for a moment. He had agreed, but he had pointed to the problems.

Months before, the sale had been announced in the *Aberdeen-Angus Journal*; had been advertised there, and in the *Texas Livestock Journal*, the *Breeder-Stockman* and other trade papers; had been fitted into its proper place in the procession of eastern sales scheduled for September and October. And, while Deep Meadow Prince bellowed, men from as far away as Texas, and from Missouri and

Iowa, from Florida and Maryland, were checking in at sales headquarters in White Plains. There might be fifty of them there, and more on the roads in cars. It was not a matter, and Harvey Landcraft pointed this out, of hanging up a sign saying, in effect, "Closed for the day."

Many of those at the pre-sale party had been still there when Mrs. Landcraft was found dead in the stall, and when the decision to call off the sale had been reached. They had been told; it was to be hoped that most of them had been able to understand, although that was not entirely certain. Cattle people are hearty, and not a few drink heartily at parties held before sales. And there had been—Wade said, from long experience—a specially festive atmosphere about this party, which was also a little in honor of Deep Meadow Prince, most honored that year of Aberdeen-Angus bulls. Glasses had gone up and down rather frequently, as was to be expected.

A great many people had, in short, come, or were coming, a long way to buy the sons and daughters of the international grand champion. Harvey pointed this out as something which required consideration. "We can't, with her dead," Wade had said, and Alec Ballard, called into the brief conference, had agreed, had added, "Specially dead this way, Mr. Landcraft. It's not so good, you know." Harvey Landcraft had looked quickly at the big farm manager, then, and had said, after only a moment, "Yes. See what you mean, Alec."

They had sent what telegrams they could, then. In the morning, before Evelyn Merritt—who had planned to stay the night in any case, and had not, with so much to do, thought of leaving—had awakened, Wade had driven off to

White Plains and the sales headquarters. And Harvey had come into the breakfast room where Evelyn and Bonita were eating little, and had said, "Can you girls take over the telephones? They'll be ringing."

They had been ringing—the line to the house; the line listed as "Deep Meadow Farm—Barns," now switched to ring in the office in the house. Calls on the house telephone were, for the most part, to express sympathy, to suggest that "help" always so quickly, if so vaguely, offered under such circumstances. Those Bonny took. The calls Evelyn answered were, for the most part, less personal—could be answered, "Yes, it is off, I'm sorry to say. No, there isn't any new date yet. It hasn't been decided."

For all their efforts, fifteen or twenty were not reached, and came to the sale—came for the luncheon which was to have preceded it at one. Alec Ballard had taken care of those, seeing them fed, apologized to, promised prompt, and individual, notice when a new sale date was decided upon; taken, when they asked, to see the bull whose fame had turned to notoriety. But they had gone now, and the telephone rang less frequently.

Wade came into the room and stood behind her, put hands on her shoulders and drew her back against him. His hands seemed to rest her. He leaned down and kissed her forehead; he said, "Good girl."

"Finished at White Plains?" Evelyn asked, and he said he had. His voice lacked vibrancy; it was a weary voice. "Harv back yet?" he asked.

Harvey Landcraft had been making those arrangements required by death, violent or peaceful. Evelyn did not know whether he was back; she had not seen him. But he came in, then, and Bonita was with him. Harvey said, "The police are back again, for some reason. Their car's parked in the turnaround."

"Yes?" Wade said. "What do they want now?"

His voice seemed, to Evelyn, sharper than it had been, the dull notes of fatigue lessened.

Harvey Landcraft shrugged; said he didn't know.

"Apparently they're down at the barns with Ballard," he said. "Looking at the scene, probably." He paused. "Why I wouldn't know," he said. "Everybody at Carmel seemed—satisfied."

"Satisfied?" Bonita said. "Isn't that a—a funny way of putting it?"

"Come off it, Bonny," her husband said. "You know what I mean. That they've all the facts, have finished with the formalties. The funeral whenever we wish—that sort of thing."

Bonny said, "Oh, of course."

"But now they show up here," Wade said.

"I suppose they have to make out forms," Bonita said. She took a deep breath, let it out slowly. "I'm tired and tired and tired," she said. "Would it be—oh, improper or anything, if I went to sleep somewhere?" She turned to her husband. "We're not driving back today?"

Harvey Landcraft shook his head. He looked at his brother.

"Things to talk over," he said. "Where we—"

He was interrupted. A maid was at the partly opened door, tapping on it.

"There're some men," she said. "Mr. Crowley and another man. They'd like to see Mr. Landcraft." She looked from one to the other of the tall men. "Either Mr. Landcraft," she said. "Mr. Crowley's the State policeman who was here last night—one of them."

"Damn," Harvey Landcraft said. He looked again, quickly, at his brother, and Wade briefly lifted his heavy shoulders.

"Take them into the library," he said. "We'll have to see them, I suppose. Go take a nap if you want to, Bonny."

But Bonita shook her head.

"You know," Bonita said, "I don't think I'm really sleepy. I think—" She paused, looked down at Evelyn, still sitting at the desk. "I think we might tag along, don't you?" Bonita Landcraft said.

There was a note in Bonita's voice. Evelyn looked at her, and Bonita, just perceptibly, lowered white lids over brown eyes, just as imperceptibly nodded as she did so. "Don't you, Evvie?" Bonny Landcraft said, and what was in her voice was a kind of insistence. But then Bonny smiled suddenly, lightly. "Form the old hollow square," she said.

But the lightness was not real; not real as the insistence had been. They *were* to form the "hollow square" which Bonny thought so highly of. To form it against—against what? And it was then, for the first time, that Evelyn Merritt realized that now the four of them were united as they had not been before—united as—well, as Deep Meadow Farm, the Deep Meadow Herd; united in ownership and in responsibility.

"All for one and one for all," Bonita said, wearing quotation—as so often she did—as a kind of mask.

Evelyn turned and looked up at Wade Landcraft, still standing behind her.

"It does come to that, I suppose," Wade said. "Harv and I—you and Bonny—" He paused. He smiled. "We own a lot of cattle," he said, and then, as if it were part of the same thing, "She was so damn alive!"

Evelyn reached up both her hands to cover his on her shoulders.

But that, she thought, will have to come later. There will be time—quieter time—to remember how alive Margaret Landcraft had been. Now Evelyn pressed the hands under hers, pushed them gently, stood up.

"All they want is to get things squared away," Harvey Landcraft said. "Got so many lines to fill in on a form, probably." He looked at Bonita. "You and your hollow squares."

"Hang together or assuredly all hang separately," Bonita said. "B. Franklin." She considered. It was all very light now. "Approximately," she said.

But it seemed to Evelyn that still, under the lightness, Bonita was drawn tight—too tight. Well, they all were; no doubt they were all showing it. They had reason enough to be.

"They will be sending out a posse," Wade said. "Come on, if we're all going."

They all went. There was no sign in the library that a posse had been contemplated by the two men there. The younger man, in uniform, was looking out a window, and seemed to be watching a thrush which ran, twinkling on tiny legs, in search of worms. The older, heavier man was looking at the titles of books on the shelves against one of the walls. (The books, Evelyn remembered, were chiefly concerned with animal husbandry.) Why, Evelyn thought, it's Ray Crowley, and then Crowley turned.

"Hello, Ray," she said and the State trooper smiled for an instant like the boy she had gone to high school with, but then adopted formality and said, "Good afternoon, Miss Merritt." But the smile was still in his eyes, for all that. Perhaps, she thought, a State trooper doesn't use first names on duty.

"'Lo, Ray," Wade Landcraft said, "what brings you here again?"

The broad-shouldered, heavily built man had turned from the books and was looking at them. He had a square face. Perhaps, Evelyn thought, a little oaken. But the face was pleasant enough, and he spoke pleasantly enough.

"I'm afraid I do," Heimrich said, and said who he was. "Sorry it's necessary, just now but—well, there's a lot of routine, naturally."

They waited. Harvey lighted a fresh cigarette, lighted one for Bonita.

"They like things neat," Heimrich said, not identifying the they. (As how could he? Things were neat enough for anybody, or almost anybody. He wondered whether this would be mentioned.)

"At Carmel," Harvey Landcraft said, "everybody seemed to think things were neat enough, captain. Anything we can tell you, of course, but—" He ended with a shrug. He looked at his younger brother.

"Sure," Wade said. "But I don't know what, either. Prince turned mean suddenly and—well, you know what happened." His eyes narrowed momentarily. "There wasn't anything neat about it, captain," he said.

"Now Mr. Landcraft," Heimrich said. "I do realize how you're feeling, how you all must be feeling." He looked at them from very blue eyes. "I realize this is an intrusion."

"But?" Harvey said.

"We like to have things clear," Heimrich said.

"A bull turns mean and kills somebody," Harvey said. "I'd think it clear enough."

"Oh yes," Heimrich said. "But—why, Mr. Landcraft? He seems to be very gentle."

"Don't tell me," Bonita said, "that you've been questioning Prince."

Heimrich smiled faintly at that. They're all very tired, he thought. It's natural they should be. All on edge. It showed in the nervous smoking of all but the girl with deeply red hair.

"In a way," he said. "In a way Mrs. Landcraft. You are Mrs. Landcraft?" Bonita nodded. "And you're Miss Merritt," Heimrich said, and Evelyn nodded. "Mr. Ballard took us down to the barn, showed us the bull, let us push him around—that is, pat him. He seemed very—placid. A little cat brushed against him, and he didn't mind."

"He likes the cat," Wade said. "He's used to the cat."

"Yes," Heimrich said. "He was used to your mother, Mr. Landcraft. Liked her probably."

"Sure," Wade said. "All the animals—"

"Wait a minute," Harvey said, and Wade waited. "What's so unusual about a bull going bad, captain? Hell—they're famous for it. Half the cartoons you see show a bull chasing somebody."

But Wade shook his head, and Heimrich, who had seemed about to answer, looked at him.

"You see what he means," Wade told his brother. "You know something about Angus, don't you, captain?"

"Well," Heimrich said, "I'm learning. Mr. Ballard was helpful. Very helpful."

"Good," Wade said. "He told you the champ's never been mean. That Aberdeen Angus—well, that they're friendly creatures, most of them. And—what else, captain?"

"About that," Heimrich said. "That this bull is well trained—halter trained, he said, I think. Used to being handled, groomed. Doesn't even mind having his hair curled." Heimrich smiled faintly. "Has been shown a good many times, with a lot of people around, probably and—well, didn't make any false moves."

"That's right," Wade said.

"A gentle bull," Heimrich said. "That—well, that bothers me, Mr. Landcraft. Bothers me a little. Why? Mr. Ballard thinks your mother must have done something to annoy him. Annoy him a lot. But—she was with the animals a good deal, wasn't she? Knew how to handle them?"

"As well as the herdsman," Wade said. He paused. "All right," he said. "It puzzles me too, captain. We'll never know, I'm afraid. I suppose she must have done something."

"What sort of thing would you guess, Mr. Landcraft?"

Wade shrugged. He said it was hard to guess. He said, "With a big animal like that, things a small animal would mind—a dog or a cat say—he wouldn't notice had happened, probably. Of course, if he were cut or something—

I don't know. Or if there was a wound and somebody tried to treat it he might get—jumpy."

"Yes," Heimrich said. "The only trouble is—Mr. Ballard says he hasn't noticed anything wrong with the bull."

"Then it's got me," Wade said.

"And," Harvey said, "what's so damned important about it, captain? We know what did happen."

Captain Heimrich closed his blue eyes.

"Now Mr. Landcraft," he said. "Probably it isn't important, naturally. As I said, it's a matter of—"

"Neatness," Harvey said. "Can't all this wait, captain? Assuming you've got to get the record so perfect as all this?"

Heimrich opened his eyes. Again he seemed about to say something, but this time it appeared that he interrupted himself. He said, "Yes, Miss Merritt?"

Evelyn looked at him. How, she wondered, did he know that something had—well, call it "crossed her mind." Instinctively, she said, "Yes what, captain?" and there was surprise in her voice. The surprise was real; it might be, she thought, wrongly interpreted.

"I thought you had thought of something," Heimrich said, very mildly. "Had you, Miss Merritt?"

She hesitated. Then she nodded. She had—she had forgotten it and it had come back; had come back when they talked of the treating of a wound, of some cut on the animal.

"It doesn't mean anything," she said. "It can't, if there wasn't any cut or anything on Prince. And—it's just an impression anyway, captain."

"Now Miss Merritt," Heimrich said. "You may as well tell me."

"All right," she said. "An odor. Not strong in the barn with—with the other odors. When I was helping—trying to help Wade and Mr. Ballard—get Mrs.—" She broke off, started again. "Get Mrs. Landcraft out of the stall," she said. "We thought she was—just hurt a little. We didn't realize—"

"No," Heimrich said. "This odor?"

"On the—on her clothes," Evelyn said, and the whole ugly scene came back, and she stopped again. Heimrich merely waited; the others merely looked at her. "A kind of hospital odor," she said. "Antiseptic. A kind of—oh, I suppose it's carbolic, really. Something like that. If she had been putting something on Prince—something that would sting—" She stopped again.

"Yes," Heimrich said. "That's interesting, Miss Merritt. But the bull apparently wasn't hurt. However—did any of the rest of you notice this odor?"

He looked around. Harvey ground out his cigarette and shook his head. Wade was just taking a new cigarette from a pack, and shook his. "No," Bonita said. "But I wasn't there, captain."

"Probably I was wrong," Evelyn said.

"Perhaps," Heimrich agreed. "But—you don't smoke, Miss Merritt?"

Surprise was spontaneous this time. She shook her head.

"The rest of you do," Heimrich said. "Smoking a good deal dulls the sense of smell. Or does with some people, anyway. So neither of you"—he nodded toward the brothers—"might have noticed it, particularly if you had been smoking a good deal during the party. You had, probably?"

"I suppose so," Harvey said. "I don't remember particularly." He shook his head. "I don't see where it gets you, anyway," he said.

"No," Heimrich said. "Well, I don't myself. But—could you ask Mr. Ballard to come up for a minute or two, Mr. Landcraft?" He spoke to Wade. Quickly, the brothers exchanged glances. Why? Evelyn wondered, and Wade Landcraft said, "Sure, if you want him. I'll call the barn."

He went out of the room.

"Is there any reason we shouldn't all sit down?" Bonita said, and turned to Evelyn as she said it. The position was slightly anomalous; in a few weeks—if sense of propriety did not postpone things—this, presumably, would be Evelyn's house. At the moment it was without a hostess. "Of course," Evelyn said, becoming hostess pro tem. They sat. It appeared to be by chance that they grouped themselves so that Captain Heimrich was facing the others. Crowley still stood by the window, evidently feeling himself not included in the invitation.

"Oh, sit down, Ray," Evelyn said.

He sat, then, but on a straight chair.

"I suppose you and your brother will keep on with this," Heimrich said, his tone that of a man who speaks idly, filling in time. But somehow, Evelyn Merritt thought, the tone doesn't fit the man.

"We'll have to talk it over," Harvey said. "Haven't got around to it yet."

"Naturally," Heimrich said.

"Depends mostly on Wade," Harvey said. "Be up to him to carry on. I'm no commuter—anyway, it's a hell of a long commute. Also, I don't really know a damn about breeding."

"Why Harvey," Bonita said, and was looked at by her husband, offered him an expression utterly without guile.

"On Wade and Evvie, of course," Harvey said.

"Oh," Evelyn said, "on Wade. Entirely on Wade."

Heimrich nodded to that, and closed his eyes—as if, Evelyn thought, the subject had begun to bore him. But, "I'd gather he's quite keen on it," Heimrich said, more than ever as if he were filling in time. Then he opened his eyes, and they were very blue, and fixed on Evelyn.

"He's always been very interested, I think," she said. "He'd have to tell you himself, of course."

Wade was back, then. He said, "Coming right along." Harvey said, "The captain seems interested in what we're going to do about Deep Meadow. Whether we'll carry on with it."

"Why?" Wade said. Heimrich merely moved his heavy shoulders slightly, in the intimation of a shrug.

"We'll have to talk it over," Wade said. "Does it interest the police?"

There was an edge in Wade Landcraft's voice.

"Now Mr. Landcraft," Heimrich said. "I merely wondered. Your manager got me interested in the setup. You and your brother do inherit the farm, of course?"

"Sure," Wade said. "What we'll do—" He broke off. He said, "Come on in, Alec," to the big man at the door of the library. He said, "All right, captain, here he is."

Heimrich looked up at Ballard. Wade said, "Oh, sit down, Alec," and Ballard said, "Thanks," and sat down. He looked with great directness at Heimrich.

Heimrich regarded him blandly.

"Something more you want to know, captain?" Ballard said.

"A little point," Heimrich said. "First, just what did happen last night? That led you—all of you—to find Mrs. Landcraft?"

"The champ bellowed," Ballard said. "The others took it up. We all figured something was wrong, and ran." He looked at Wade Landcraft, and Landcraft said, "That's right, captain."

Heimrich nodded. He said, "Go on, Mr. Landcraft."

Wade went on, speaking slowly. He had been on the lawn, with the guests. There were still perhaps a hundred people on the lawn, around the bar, sitting at tables, talking. He had moved around among them.

"So did I," Harvey said.

"You saw each other from time to time?"

"Sure," Wade said.

"And your mother."

"Yes. Obviously she left, but I didn't notice when. Did you?" The last was to his brother. Harvey Landcraft shook his head.

"I was sitting on the terrace," Evelyn said. "Bonny and I were sitting on the terrace, just—resting. Doing nothing."

"No," Bonny said. "I'd gone in. Don't you remember? To—shall I say powder my nose, captain? I was still inside when—" She broke off. "I was still inside," she said.

"Oh yes," Evelyn said. "I do remember."

"And the bulls started bellowing," Heimrich said.

"I was in one of the other barns," Ballard said. "I'd

been showing somebody around—don't remember the man's name. He came back up here. I'd started back and one of the men stopped me to ask about something—something about what he was to do during the sale. Then—"

Then the big bull had bellowed and the others had taken it up. On the terrace, people sitting, people standing, looked toward the barns; people stood up, looked down toward the lights in the barns.

"The barns were lighted?" Heimrich asked.

There had been bulbs burning in the barns, bulbs lighted over the doors.

Harvey and Wade Landcraft had, when the bellowing went on, increased, started toward the barns. After a few seconds, they were running. Several of the guests had, after a little, run after them; Evelyn, seeing the Landcrafts starting, realizing something was wrong, had run across the lawn, among the people, after them.

"And you, Mr. Ballard?"

He had run through the barn he was in, across the yard between barns, into the barn which housed Deep Meadow Prince. "Knew he'd started it," Ballard said. "Got there about the same time the rest did."

The Landcrafts, one or two other men, Evelyn Merritt, had come into the barn from the end closest the house; Ballard from the other end. There was general agreement that the brothers and Ballard had arrived at about the same time. The bull was in the center of the stall, then, still bellowing. He faced what was in the corner of the stall, lying on the straw.

Ballard had silenced the bull, slapped him away. Prince

had quietened without difficulty. They had got Mrs. Landcraft out, found her dead.

"Who?" Heimrich asked.

It was not clear who first had reached Mrs. Landcraft; nobody could be sure. There had been, or at any rate now remained, no clarity about the brief, hurried, frightening scene in the big bull's stall. The three men had lifted the dead woman; Evelyn, a second or two later, had helped; had knelt beside her on the paved floor of the barn—knelt with the brothers, found nothing to be done.

"It must have been then," Heimrich said, "that you detected this odor, Miss Merritt."

Evelyn nodded, said she supposed it had been then.

"An odor like disinfectant," Heimrich said. "A hospital odor. When you were beside the body?"

"Yes."

"You didn't notice that, Mr. Ballard?"

"I don't—" Ballard began, and paused. "There's usually a little of that around the barns," he said. "We keep them clean. Can't say I noticed—" He broke off again, and slightly narrowed his eyes. "Come to think of it, maybe I did," he said. "Anyway, it'd fit in because—I was just going to call you, Mr. Landcraft, when you called me. Prince's got a scratch on his right hind leg on the outside. Nothing to bother with but—somebody's put stuff on it. I didn't, and Smitty didn't."

He looked from Wade Landcraft to Captain Heimrich.

"Told you I hadn't found anything wrong with the champ," Ballard said. "I didn't when I looked him over last night. But, with things the way they were, I didn't look very carefully. After you came up here, I did—found this scratch. Guess that explains the whole thing, mister."

"Does it?" Heimrich said.

"Well, it could. Mrs. Landcraft noticed the scratch for some reason. Maybe she had been showing the champ off to somebody. Saw it hadn't been treated, and decided to put something on it. Used full strength, the stuff we use stings. Maybe Prince jumped and kicked her and then, when she fell or something—started to try to get out of the stall, anyhow—went for her. Probably the can she had the stuff in spilled on her, and maybe when he kicked her there was—well, blood. The two things together'd be likely to start him off." He turned toward Wade. "You know that, Mr. Landcraft," he said.

Wade Landcraft looked at the farm manager, then at Heimrich. He nodded, slowly. He said the odors might, at that.

"So there you are, mister," Ballard said. "I wouldn't have thought of it, I guess, if you hadn't come—if you hadn't wanted to look the place over."

"Hadn't come nosing around," he had started to say, Heimrich reflected. A reasonable enough description, too; understandable enough.

"There's only one point," Heimrich said. "This—disinfectant—something like iodine, probably? Merthiolate? Whatever it was, there has to be a container, naturally. A bottle? A can?"

"Screw top can," Ballard said. "You're right there, mister. Be in the stall somewhere, wouldn't it?"

"Now Mr. Ballard," Heimrich said. "I'd think so, naturally."

"Sure it would," Ballard said. "You know—I'll bet it is.

Pretty near got to be—down in the straw somewhere. Because—"

He turned to Wade.

"Haven't got around to changing it yet," he said, and his tone was apologetic. "So damn many things going on. Figured when we put him out tonight would be time enough." He turned back to Hemrich. "Didn't turn him out last night because people wanted to look at him," he explained.

Heimrich raised his eyebrows. He was told that, when the weather was warm, as it was then, the big bull spent his days in the comparative coolness of the barn, under fans; his nights in a paddock. "Usually with a bull calf to play with," Ballard said. "Keeps him from getting sluggish."

Cattle would distract the big farm manager from anything, Heimrich thought; violent death was incidental to the nurturing of giant bulls. The Landcrafts, evidently, had a conscientious man in big Alec Ballard.

"Yes," Heimrich said. "Would it do him any harm if he were turned out to the paddock now, Mr. Ballard? And the straw changed? Because if we find the container it will clear things up, naturally."

Ballard looked at Wade Landcraft. To him, he said, "Wouldn't hurt the champ, Mr. Landcraft."

It seemed to Evelyn that Wade hesitated perceptibly, that—for no reason which came quickly to the mind—he looked at his brother before he answered. But when he answered, it was to say, "Sure, Alec. May as well get things cleared up, since the captain feels there's something—" He turned to Heimrich then. "What *do* you feel, captain?"

he said, and again his voice was edged. "You suspect something?"

"Now Mr. Landcraft," Heimrich said. "I told you. We like to have things neat. They want everything explained. That's all it is." He smiled. "Afraid we don't know as much about cattle as you people do," he said. "But if it's not too much trouble, we might as well find the container. As long as Crowley and I are here."

He stood up, then, and the others stood. But there was, Heimrich pointed out, no need to trouble any of them but Ballard; he had troubled everyone too much already. He appreciated the patience of all of them—of Mr. Landcraft *and* Mr. Landcraft, of Mrs. Landcraft and Miss Merritt. Once they'd finished at the barn, found the container—as he had no doubt they would—they would be on their way.

It seemed to Evelyn Merritt that, with that, a certain tension departed. She had been only partially conscious that there had been tension—only something in Wade's voice had been tangible. It was odd, and a little disturbing, to find how conscious she now was of a general relaxation. They were all, she thought, glad to see this solid, unhurried man on the point of leaving. Well, that meant nothing—she was herself. It was merely that they had all been under strain, grown tired under strain.

They're all very glad to see me go, Heimrich thought, going with Ballard, with Crowley behind them. It was most natural that they should be. They had been up most of the night, were physically and emotionally tattered. And then, for no apparent reason, an enquiring policeman had come. It was to be expected that Wade Landcraft should not quite hide his impatience; that his older—and rather more experienced—brother should just contain his; that the young and pretty Mrs. Landcraft should light and stub out, light and stub out, cigarette after cigarette. Evelyn Merritt had been very conscious of Wade Landcraft's edginess—had seemed, at times, almost worried about him. Well, it was to be presumed she was in love with him, since she was on the verge of marrying him. She would be concerned about him.

They walked down the sloping lawn to the first of the white barns. Heimrich and Crowley waited while Ballard, aided by another man—by Smith, William Smith, the herdsman—haltered the great bull and led him from the stall, through a door, into a railed paddock outside. The bull passed, very docilely, within a few feet of Heimrich; the scratch on one of his short hind legs was, now that he was no longer standing in deep straw, easily seen. It was not, Heimrich thought, a serious scratch, particularly for so large an animal.

"Not much hurt," Heimrich said, to the young trooper, and pointed to the scratch. "A little thing to cause what it seems to have caused."

"That's right, sir," Crowley said. "That's—" He stopped speaking; he looked at Heimrich.

Heimrich nodded slowly. He said it was, of course, a very small thing.

With the bull gone, Smith ran a tractor into the barn, dragging a hay cart behind it. He and another man forked straw from the stall to the cart, shaking each forkful carefully. They were almost down to the cement floor when metal tinkled against the tines of a fork.

The can was almost flattened; the label half torn off. Ballard picked it up, handed it to Heimrich.

"He's been standing on it," Ballard said, and it was clear Prince had been standing on it. The odor of antiseptic was very evident, emanating from the can.

"Well," Ballard said. "I guess that does it, mister."

"Yes, Mr. Ballard," Heimrich said. "I guess that does it."

They went, then. When they were in the car, before Crowley started it, Heimrich asked a question.

"How long ago would you think the bull was scratched, Crowley?"

"Twelve hours or so," Ray Crowley said. "At the outside."

"At the outside," Heimrich said. "Probably rather less. Perhaps a good deal less. Still dried blood on the hair. Notice that? He'd been standing in straw, moving around, naturally. Dried blood would rub off."

"Yes," Trooper Crowley said.

"I'm afraid," Captain Heimrich said, "that somebody's played rather a dirty trick on the bull, aren't you, Ray?"

V

Still there were things to do, things to be seen to, to be decided. But for some time after Heimrich went out of the house with Alec Ballard, the four sat where he had left them, doing nothing and saying little. They had hurried and hurried, Evelyn thought; had been driven and so hard driven that there had been no time for thought. Now she must pull herself together, get her car, drive home. But she did not pull herself together, nor, for a long time, say anything about going home. There was a feeling of incompleteness in her mind; an impression that, before she went, there was something which she would have to do.

"What gets you," Wade said in the silence, after it had persisted for many minutes—"what gets you, is that she loved that bull. You know what I mean?"

He looked at Evelyn, rather than at the others, and Evelyn nodded and said, "Yes, Wade," and only then, after she had spoken, realized that she did know what he meant—what he meant by Margaret Landcraft's "love" for the big bull. You could call it that; she had liked to stand and look at him, and it was not all—it was not even chiefly—that he represented, in addition to money, a special kind of triumph, a kind of culmination. Margaret Landcraft, Evelyn thought, had looked at the bull so long, so often, because he was, in himself, so perfect an animal. Evelyn had herself felt that, and she knew of the Blacks only what she had been told. With a breeder's special knowledge, Mrs. Landcraft must have felt the animal's perfection with far greater intensity. But probably it had been more, even than that—and perhaps the word "love" was only an approximation. To some very considerable extent, Margaret Landcraft's life must have centered around the black bull which had killed her.

And what I feel now, Evelyn thought, illumination coming rather suddenly, is the lack of a center here, in this house; what I am waiting for, have been waiting for, is for her to come into the room, and take over the room and—when I have thanked her as a guest—release me.

"It's hard to realize she won't walk in," Harvey said, and Evelyn was startled for a moment to find their thoughts so parallel, but then realized there was nothing startling about it—thought that they had all, in some fashion, been waiting for the big, the indomitable, woman to take charge.

"This gets us no place. We all need a drink," Wade said, then, and his voice was louder than before, and when Evelyn said that, on the other hand, she ought to be thinking of going home, he said, "Nonsense. Anyway, we've all got to talk," and went out of the library. "You've been told," Bonita said, from the depths of a chair, her voice tired.

She had, in a way, Evelyn thought—and found that, with the thought, she felt lighter, as if she had begun to come out from under something.

"Funny thing about the cops," Harvey Landcraft said a

little later, while they still waited for Wade to return with the drink tray. "Hadn't realized they went to so much trouble." He paused for a moment. "In the country," he added.

"You make it," Bonita said, "sound like the African veldt." Her voice trailed off a little. "Not that they aren't particular on the veldt, probably," she added.

"Particular?" her husband repeated.

Bonita merely looked at him; Evelyn felt that some acknowledgement passed between them—acknowledgement of a thought shared. But Harvey seemed to deny that, shaking his head sharply. Wade came back, then, carrying a tray of bottles and glasses, and Alec Ballard came after him, with a deep ice bucket. Ballard was unexpected; his presence underlined the change in the house. Yet the emphasis was subtle. Ballard was often in the house; he was often, of necessity, in the office. But it was, nevertheless, surprising that he appeared, now, to be coming in to have a drink with them.

"Well," Wade said, and put the tray down. "They found the can. The can mother must have been using. Went away satisfied, apparently." He looked at Alec Ballard and the big man put the ice container down on the floor by the table on which Wade had put the tray, and then stood up and nodded, slowly.

"Never any reason they shouldn't have been," Harvey said, with emphasis.

"Sure not, Mr. Landcraft," Alec Ballard said. "Young cop trying to make a name for himself."

But that was wrong, Evelyn thought. Ray Crowley wasn't a young policeman over-animated by zeal. Or, she didn't think he was. He was a boy she had gone to high school with; a quiet boy, prone to thinking things out quietly. Ballard made him sound—

"He looked like a nice boy to me," Bonita said, and then Ballard said, "Sure. Didn't mean he wasn't, Mrs. Landcraft."

"Anyway, they've gone," Wade said. "So that's that." He began to put ice in glasses. "Thought Ballard might as well be in on it," he said, and began to pour on ice, to hand drinks to Evelyn, to Bonita, finally to his brother. He filled two more, one for Ballard, and turned to face them.

"What it comes to," he said, "is, I'd like to see the herd sold off." He said that to all of them; to Evelyn he said, "That all right, Evvie?" He waited.

"It's fine, Wade," she said, and smiled up at him. She felt a special lightness. "I think you're right." He nodded, just perceptibly, and now an unspoken sharing was between them, as it had been between Bonita and Harvey.

"It's as much up to you as to me," Wade said, and now to his brother—and to Bonny. "Maybe you want to step in, Harv?"

"God forbid," Harvey said, and Bonita, smiling a little, shook her head. "So very far from Madison," she said. "So many miles from Fifty-Second Street."

"Also," Harvey said, "it's not my line. Of course, I suppose if Alec stayed on—"

Ballard was sitting on a straight chair. He looked at Harvey, then at Wade. It was impossible, Evelyn thought, to tell from his face what he thought. He merely waited.

"The catch is this," Wade said. "There wouldn't be a

great deal of money—not a great deal coming out. That's right, Alec?"

"Not if you want to keep it going," Alec Ballard said. "Going as it should. We're—we were—still expanding. What came out had to go back, mostly. Your mother wanted it that way, Mr. Landcraft. It's the only way if you want—well, the kind of herd she wanted. I don't say she didn't get in the black this last year, but—"

"A few thousand," Wade said. "Over and above everything—Alec's salary, mine—the whole works. She'd have used it for more stock. That would have made sense but—she was interested. I'm not. You're not, Harv. Evvie and I—well, we'd rather do something else. So—" He looked at his brother, at his brother's wife. "We don't have to decide today," he said. "But it'll make a difference to several people—Alec here, for example."

"We may as well decide today," Harvey said. "I'm with you on selling. Sooner the better since—" He did not finish, although he was given time.

It could not, unless they were very lucky, be very soon, Wade said, and Ballard nodded agreement. The chance of getting a single buyer, for farm and herd, was remote. They might sell the big bull by private treaty, for the rest—Wade then seemed to hand it to Ballard. They already had talked about it, Evelyn thought.

"Hold a dispersion in the spring," Ballard said. "No use trying sooner—have to get word around, advertise it. We'll get a crowd and if they feel like buying—" He ended with a shrug. "May have to put Prince in, at that," he said. He shook his head. "That'll be something," he said. "International grand champion to the highest bidder. Nothing like that, before."

"How much would we be likely to get?" Harvey asked.

Ballard shook his head again. He said he couldn't guess. Yesterday—

"Yesterday we didn't want to disperse," he said. "And—yesterday Prince wasn't a mean bull. About a third of the animals weren't offspring of a mean bull. What that'll do to—"

"I still don't think he's a mean one," Wade said.

"Sure," Ballard said. "Something hurt him, he kicked out without thinking, and spilled this stuff—hates the smell of the stuff, like all of 'em—gets to lurching around. Don't prove he's mean, or's bred meanness into his get. But—who's going to work it out that way? Specially when they can get bargains?"

"He's right, Harv," Wade said. "We won't get what we ought to. But—we'll get a good deal."

"That's right," Ballard said. "And, if you don't want to run the place, or hire somebody to run it—and it seems you don't—what choice've you got? What—" He stopped, because a maid had appeared at the library door. She carried a large envelope. She said, to Wade, "I'm sorry, Mr. Landcraft, but a man left this and said you'd want to see it as soon as possible." Wade held out a hand, she crossed the room and gave him the envelope, which was large, and heavy, to which was clipped a note.

"I don't know what we'll do with these, under the circumstances," the note said. "Maybe they'll want to call the whole thing off, maybe they'll rush it through. Anyway, we said you could see them first. We'd like to pick them up tomorrow." The note was signed with initials, quite indecipherable. The envelope held glossy photographs of people and of black cattle, *Life* magazine's record of the pre-sale party of Deep Meadow Farm. Abstractedly, Wade looked for a place to put the envelope, ended by handing it to Evelyn.

"There ought," Harvey said, "to be a way to get word around about what did happen—keep people from thinking we've got a mean bull to sell."

They would, Wade said, naturally try to do that. But—he spread his hands slightly. They couldn't prove anything. People would believe what they wanted to—and what paid them best. Perhaps they would believe the bull had merely become excited, but why would they admit the belief, if a belief in his meanness kept prices down?

Harvey Landcraft supposed he was right. They had a scratched bull, a battered can which had contained an antiseptic solution. "Maybe," he said, "we ought to take pictures of the can and the scratch." This was not, his tone said, to be taken seriously; it was not so taken. But then Ballard said, "Don't know about the can, Mr. Landcraft. Smitty probably threw it away, unless—" He stopped.

"You know," he said, "I gave it to that policeman—the captain—to look at. I don't remember as he gave it back."

It was an odd remark to cause a sudden stillness in the room. The stillness was penetrating, like a cold wind; it was heavy, like a weight.

Wade said nothing in the stillness, but he reached for the photographs Evelyn still held. Then the silence was broken—by the rattle of the envelope being opened, then by the soft hissing of smooth photographs being slid one over another. And then that faint sound stopped. Wade looked at the photograph he held, looked at it carefully, held it to the light, looked at the back. Then, without speaking, he handed it to Evelyn.

It was an excellent photograph of Deep Meadow Prince, taken in profile. As Evelyn held the picture up to look at it, the bull faced her right hand. She looked up from the picture at Wade Landcraft.

"Turn it over," he said.

She turned it over. Lightly in pencil she read: "20 min before accident."

"Show the others," Wade said, and she handed the picture to Harvey Landcraft, who was nearest. After a moment he handed it to his wife.

"I don't—" Bonita said, and stopped, and then said, very slowly, *"There isn't any, is there?"*

It was a very clear picture; it had been taken, not in the stall, where the bull stood deep in straw, but on the smooth floor. It was a very clear picture of all the bull, including his right hind leg—a leg glossy and unscratched, like the rest of him.

VI

ANYWAY, HEIMRICH WAS told in the Putnam County Court House in Carmel—anyway, he had come up with a new one. "Biggest blunt object I ever heard of," the district attorney said. "A ton or so of bull, used as a murder weapon." He shook his head. "I'd just as soon not take that one to court," he said. "Particularly in dairy country."

He was looking ahead, Heimrich told him—he was looking a long way ahead. As to the novelty of the method—"if it was the method, naturally"—novelty was always relative. Murder, planned, long premeditated, had been committed with motor cars as weapons; he knew of a case in which a man—a smallish man, to be sure—had been fatally merged with hay in a baling machine. As for animals—wild dogs had been used in earlier days; lions were, historically, well regarded as executioners by the Romans. For all Heimrich knew, bulls might have been used often before.

"Bulls with horns," the district attorney said. "Maybe." He added that Heimrich did not, so far as he could see, have much to go on. He added, to that, that it was, of course, up to Heimrich.

"But this tin can," he said. "The fact—if it is a fact—that the animal was scratched *after* Mrs. Landcraft was dead. And what good's the can? Your prints on it. Ballard's prints on it. He handed it to you, so his prints have to be. You took it, so yours have to be. And there's nothing else but smudges. Nothing to show Mrs. Landcraft didn't handle it."

"I know," Heimrich said.

"Suppose you're an expert on wounds," the district attorney said, and Heimrich said, "Oh, I am in a way, naturally. Crowley agrees, too."

"Suppose you are," the attorney said. "Suppose you both are. You see this scratch as the animal walks by, Crowley guesses twelve hours, you guess less. By now—by tomorrow, anyway—the best vet in the world couldn't put it within twenty-four hours. Not and make it stick. You realize that?"

"Oh yes," Heimrich said. "I realize that."

"You say somebody—I suppose you think Ballard—"

"Not necessarily," Heimrich said. "Anybody on the farm would have had the opportunity—the Landcrafts, the girls. The herdsman. Anyone who had been at the party and—hung around."

"Whoever it was," the attorney said. "You think someone scratched the animal, after the woman's death, to provide an explanation if somebody got—well, got nosy. Keeping a jump ahead, providing for contingencies."

"Yes," Heimrich said. "I do think that."

"But," the attorney said, "can't prove it."

"No. Not now."

"Or anything else."

"Not yet."

"What you're up against is the how," the attorney said. "Suppose I want to make a bull kill somebody I want killed. But suppose the bull is gentle—used to people, like this Deep Meadow Prince. The kind of bull you lead around by halter; the kind of bull likes to have his nose rubbed. You say he does?"

"Seemed to," Heimrich said. "Likes his forehead scratched, too."

"All right," the attorney said. "This—this milk-toast. How do I get him to kill this somebody I want killed? Somebody the bull knows, remember; somebody he's used to; somebody who's used to bulls."

"I don't know," Heimrich said. He added, "Yet."

"It's up to you," the attorney said. "I'd drop it, myself."

"No," Heimrich said. "I don't think so, counsellor. The woman was murdered. The bull was used. We can't drop it."

"All right," the attorney said. "I don't see where you even get started, but all right."

"Oh," Heimrich said, "I start around the edges, naturally."

He went to the office of the medical examiner. There were two points, one simple. Yes, obviously, Mrs. Landcraft could have been knocked unconscious and put into the stall with the bull. The doctor had seen nothing to indicate this; nothing to render it impossible. "She was pretty much a mass of contusions when I saw her. The bull might have made any of them. So, I suppose, might a club. Nothing to prove it, though. She'd been banged against the wall and the wooden rails, so wood splinters wouldn't help. Even if there were any. I didn't see any, as I recall."

Heimrich nodded.

"One other thing," he said. "Earlier—when I was here first—you suggested she might have been treating the bull. Putting something on him. I asked what made you think of that, and you couldn't put a finger on it. I wonder if you can now?"

The physician shrugged. He said Heimrich had appeared to want an explanation. He'd offered one that seemed reasonable. That was the only "finger" he could put on it.

"When you examined the body," Heimrich said. "Was there an odor on the clothing? An odor of, say—"

But the physician snapped his fingers. He said, "There you've got the subconscious." He said, "Sure I did—odor of antiseptic. Didn't think of it afterward, or didn't know I thought of it. But—you've hit on it, captain. I remembered subconsciously and came up with this theory. Things like that do make you wonder if—"

"Yes," Heimrich said. "Well, that clears that up. Somebody else noticed the odor, you see. Makes it all very neat, naturally."

"Listen," the doctor said, "you think it wasn't?"

"Oh," Heimrich said. "Neat enough, in its way. As murder goes."

The doctor's eyebrows climbed, precariously.

"Well, thanks, doctor," Heimrich said. He went.

He went to a telephone. He called the office of two attorneys, both in Brewster, either of whom might, the district attorney had thought, have drawn up a will for Mrs. Margaret Landcraft. The first had not. The second evidently had, although he was careful. How did he know Heimrich was Heimrich? What passed between attorney and client was—

Heimrich sighed. He asked the attorney to stand by. He telephoned the district attorney. The district attorney telephoned the attorney in Brewster. Heimrich telephoned the attorney in Brewster.

"Yes," the Brewster man said, "I did, captain. Very simple will. Leaves everything to her sons, share and share alike."

"Thanks, counsellor," Heimrich said.

He went out of the court house then, and stood for some minutes on a sidewalk, looking across a pretty lake, which sparkled in the lowering sun. It was still very warm, as September often is. There was haze in the air; the still green trees—except for the ashes, already spitting their brown leaves to earth—were motionless. It was five minutes before Trooper Crowley picked the captain up.

Crowley had been to the Brewster barracks. He was in civilian clothes—in gray slacks and a tweed jacket. He looked not at all like a policeman; he looked like a summer resident who had, inexplicably, tarried beyond Labor Day. The car he drove was a sedan, unidentified as a police car. When you nibbled around the edges, there was no point in advertising it to anyone who might see a police car parked—parked, for example, in the driveway of a country veterinarian's house and office; parked beyond a sign which read: "James Nugent, D.V.S."

Dr. Nugent was in his office. He was a gray-haired man of medium size, with the face of a countryman. He wore a gray suit. He smoked a pipe. He said, "Hello, Ray. Sick cow?"

"Not this time, doc," Ray said. "This is Captain Heimrich."

Dr. Nugent stood part way up and extended a hand and sat down again. He said, "Captain, eh? Same outfit?"

"Same outfit," Heimrich said.

"On business, then?"

"Well," Heimrich said, "you can call it that, doctor. You take care of the animals at Deep Meadow Farm?"

Dr. Nugent removed his pipe. He looked thoughtfully at Heimrich.

"So that's the way the wind blows," he said. "Yes, I do, captain. Very fine stock. Very great bull."

"And from all I hear," Heimrich said, "usually a very gentle bull."

"Yes," Nugent said. "They're mostly very gentle, beef bulls. Not much meanness in them. Dairy bulls, that's another matter. Them you can't trust."

"And this one—Deep Meadow Prince—was healthy?"

Nugent raised eyebrows. He nodded his gray head briskly. He waited.

"I'm trying to find out how this happened," Heimrich said. "Why it happened. It occurred to me that—well, people get nervous and irritable when they're not well. Sometimes they do. It occurred to me—perhaps cattle do too. Might make them spiteful."

Dr. Nugent nodded.

"Might," he said. "Does, sometimes."

"But this bull was healthy?"

"I haven't looked at him for a month or so," Dr. Nugent said. "In fine shape then. Ballard thought he was getting too heavy, wanted to fine him down a bit. Some breeders like them heavy as they'll get, others don't. Ballard wanted me to check before he put him—well, on a reducing diet. I never saw a healthier animal."

"A month or so ago, you say?"

Nugent nodded.

"But," he said, "if there'd been any trouble, I'd have seen him since. Ballard's a good man; knows enough to call the doctor. And they didn't call in another veterinarian. I'd have—heard."

"The bull seems to have got scratched, somehow."

"Does he? Much of a scratch?"

It wasn't, Heimrich said. He described it.

"Probably snagged on a barb," Nugent said. "Ballard treated it?"

"Somebody did."

"Nothing to worry about then," Nugent said. "Happens often enough. What gets them is pneumonia. Or something the matter with their insides." He nodded, as if to himself. "They die easy then, for such big animals," he said. "Don't seem to make much of a fight. A dog, now—he'll fight hard. A cow, no. Sometimes you'd think they just said, 'The hell with it.'" He stopped. "Not what you want," he said. "I get to talking. Old age, probably."

Dr. Nugent was, Heimrich judged, in his middle fifties. He looked very healthy to Heimrich.

"Being on this diet," Heimrich said. "Might that make

him edgy? It does people." He paused. "I've heard," he said.

"Shouldn't think so," Dr. Nugent said. "You've seen him?"

Heimrich nodded.

"Strike you as upset? Edgy?"

Deep Meadow Prince had struck Heimrich as exceedingly placid. Heimrich said so.

"Then I don't know," Nugent said. "Dieting oughtn't to have bothered him. After all, he hasn't lost more than a couple of hundred pounds. Perhaps not even that."

Dr. Nugent shook his head. He relighted his pipe.

"Why did he turn on Mrs. Landcraft, doctor?"

"Probably because she hurt him," Nugent said. "Put something on this scratch. Wasn't careful."

It was the familiar story. Heimrich shook his head to it. He said he doubted it.

"I'm afraid," Nugent said, emitting smoke, "that it's all I've got to offer, captain. You want more?"

"Yes," Heimrich said. "I do want more. A gentle animal. All at once he—hates. Kills. A person he knew. That is—I don't suppose he had a grudge against Mrs. Landcraft?"

Nugent laughed briefly. He shook his head.

"No grudge against anybody I know of," he said. "Except me, of course."

Heimrich closed his eyes. He waited a second. He said, "Now doctor. Against you?"

"They all hate me," Nugent said. "The calves do, pretty early. The cows do. The bulls do. But so do horses and cats. Now and then you get a dog's different, but not often. Stands to reason—but still—" He emitted further smoke.

"Funny thing is," he said, "I rather like animals. How I got into this." He indicated his office.

Heimrich opened his eyes, looked at Nugent.

"Oh," Nugent said, "nothing against me personally, far as I know. They hate all veterinarians. It stands to reason, as I said. We hurt them, so they hate us. Can't tell a cow it's all for her own good. Can't help hurting them. For one thing, they all get shots. At a place like the Landcrafts', anyway. Now and then we have to operate, and we don't give anesthetics to cattle. I don't, anyway. Nobody knows exactly how much to give, so it's chancy and—" He stopped.

"You don't want all that," he said.

"I don't know," Heimrich said. "However—does this bull hate you enough to—go for you?"

"If he thought he could get away with it," Nugent said. "We see he doesn't, of course. Even if he is too big to hoist."

Heimrich merely shook his head.

"Smaller animals we put in stocks," Nugent said. "Put a belly band under them. Hoist up. When we want to trim their feet, say. The champ's too big. We can put him in a squeeze, if we have to. Never have, but we could." He looked at Heimrich. "Just a gadget to keep 'em from jumping around," he said.

"Look, doctor," Heimrich said. "He gets this way—wants to go for you—only when you're doing something he doesn't like? Like giving him a shot? Other times—"

"Other times he keeps right on hating me," Nugent said.

"He know you by sight, you mean?"

Nugent hesitated. He relighted his pipe. He said, "I don't know why I keep on smoking these damn things."

He said, "It amounts to that, but probably's not that. They make associations. All animals do. Friend of mine in New York. Small-animal man. Cat man, primarily. He used to have a mannerism—whenever he called at a house, or an apartment, he'd ring the doorbell twice, fast. Like a mail carrier. So—they'd let him in and he'd go to the apartment and—no cats. Take them an hour to find one cat. One place he went had three cats. Used to take three hours. He quit ringing that way, and they quit hiding. Association." He emitted smoke. "Of course," he said, "they kept on hiding whenever anybody else rang that way. Association persisted."

Heimrich had closed his eyes again. He kept them closed. When he spoke, it seemed to be with care.

"Now doctor," he said, "I want to get this straight. Something about you sets up an association in the minds of—well, cattle, which is what we're talking about. Specifically, this big bull of the Landcrafts'. So—he goes for you. With these cats in the city, and your friend, it was a sequence of sounds. With you—what? Your voice?"

"No," Nugent said. "It's the same whether I speak or not. It's the way I smell."

Heimrich opened his eyes. Involuntarily, he sniffed. He smelled pipe smoke. And James Nugent, doctor of veterinary surgery, laughed.

"No," he said. "Not the pipe. I don't work in these clothes. The clothes I do work in smell of medicine, of course. Of antiseptics. If I've been operating, or anything like that, often of blood. I smell like a hospital, animal or human. First time I inoculate a calf, it gets hurt. At the same time, it gets this hospital smell. Association. Even you and I have odor associations, and we're hardly able to smell at all. Imagine what it is for a cat or dog."

"Or—a bull," Heimrich said.

Nugent's pipe had gone out again. He looked at it; he shook his head; he put his pipe in a tray. He nodded his head. "Or a bull," he said. Then, looking at Heimrich, the veterinarian's eyes suddenly narrowed. "Or a bull," he repeated.

"These cats you mentioned," Heimrich said. "You say the association persisted even when it didn't apply? Even when the person who rang twice was—oh, a delivery boy? The mail carrier?"

"Yes," Nugent said. "It was all the same to the cats, of course. A certain sound meant this vet—this veterinarian—they hated. They hid."

"And a certain odor?"

"Yes," Nugent said. He spoke slowly. "Yes, I'd think so, captain. I'd think that if, say, Mrs. Landcraft had smelled to Prince like a veterinarian—like me—he might have gone for her. I'd have thought she'd have a good chance of getting away, of course. She was an active woman for her age. The bull is a little—cumbersome. Particularly when he's in a stall."

"Now doctor," Heimrich said. "If she'd been conscious, naturally. Suppose she'd been knocked out first? With a club or a blackjack. Put in the stall."

Nugent picked up his pipe and looked at it, as if he were seeking to determine how it had been made, what its purpose was. He spoke without looking away from the pipe.

"I'd have propped her up in a corner of the stall," he said. "Look more natural to the bull, that way. Then, if it had been necessary, I'd have reached over and jabbed him with a needle."

"It would have worked?"

Nugent looked at Heimrich now; looked at him very steadily.

"I suppose something had been spilled on her clothes?" Nugent said. "Antiseptic? Something smelling of carbolic? And perhaps a little blood, too? After she'd been knocked out, I suppose?"

"That would have been the time, naturally," Heimrich said. "Would it have worked?"

"Yes, captain," Dr. Nugent said. "I don't think there's any doubt it would have worked." He paused. "You think it did," he said, and this was not a question.

Heimrich nodded.

"Who?" the doctor asked.

"Now doctor," Heimrich said. "I don't know that—yet." He stood up.

"I don't know enough about the people," he said. "I'll have to find out, naturally. Mrs. Landcraft was dangerous to somebody. Or had something somebody wanted. Can you help?"

"No," Nugent said. "I can't help you there."

"Who might?"

"You go roundabout," Nugent said.

"To start with," Heimrich said. "You see, there isn't any murder, doctor. No obvious murder. Were you there last night, doctor? At the Landcraft party?"

"For a time," Nugent said. He picked up his pipe and began to scrape it out into the ash tray. "I left before this happened. I didn't hear until this morning." He pushed the pipe into a jar of tobacco and began to cram with a thumb. "Florence Haskins knew Margaret better than most," he said. "She's a breeder too. Got a place up in Dutchess. You know it, don't you, Ray?"

Ray Crowley said, "Yes, doc. Sure."

"Florrie was there last night," Nugent said. "She knows about everybody in the business. She and Margaret went to sales together, pretty often. Talked of going shares on a bull they came across last spring. Don't know that they ever did." He lighted the pipe. "Might be worth your while to talk to Florrie, captain," he said and, with his pipe fuming again, stood up. "She likes to talk."

"About my dinner time," he said. "Anything else, captain?"

There was not. He was thanked.

It was about everybody's dinner time. Ray Crowley knew a place near Brewster, and they ate there. It was growing dark when they finished. Crowley looked at Heimrich in enquiry.

"In the morning, Ray," Heimrich said. "In the morning." The younger man looked, Heimrich thought, disappointed. "Oh," Heimrich said, "I'll want you along, naturally. I'll get you assigned."

the [illegible] full [illegible] of [illegible], [illegible] with
[illegible] than
[illegible]
[illegible] know it, don't you?"
[illegible]
[illegible] August? [illegible]
[illegible]
[illegible] of going [illegible]
[illegible] Don't know that [illegible]
[illegible]
[illegible] Toronto [illegible]
[illegible] stood up. She [illegible]
[illegible] anything [illegible]
[illegible]

[illegible]
[illegible] time [illegible]
[illegible] It was
[illegible]
[illegible]

[illegible]
[illegible]
[illegible] all.
[illegible]

[illegible]

VII

Bonita Landcraft had said, "Well, I guess we do form a hollow square, at that," and there had been no lightness in her voice; her voice said that whatever jest there had once been in the phrase had been wrung out of it. She had said that three hours before and now—save that dinner had been eaten, lights turned on—they had got little further. It was Wade who summed it up for the four of them, sitting again in the library.

"All we know is that it wasn't the way we thought," Wade said.

But Harvey Landcraft shook his head. They knew, or could be almost certain, of one thing more than that—the police, also, did not think that loose ends were neatly tied. They could be sure, for one thing, that the police captain—he snapped his fingers and Bonny supplied the name—that Captain Heimrich had taken with him the flattened can which had held antiseptic solution. They could guess—had to guess—he had taken it in the hope he would find fingerprints on it. And what that meant was obvious.

"For one thing," Bonita said, "that he'll be back." Then she put it flatly. "He thinks Mother Landcraft was murdered," Bonita said, and light from a lamp made shadows on her young face, so that it seemed older, seemed almost haggard.

"We don't know that," Evelyn heard herself saying. "Nobody knows that—we don't know anything."

"That somebody tried to make them seem a certain way—an innocent way," Harvey said. "That we know. The reason is obvious—what did happen wasn't innocent."

"If we believe Smith," Wade said. "If, in the end, everybody believes Smith."

There had been that one obvious path of escape from the ugly implication of the photograph. It, from the notation, had been taken twenty minutes before the bull killed his owner. If he had not been scratched in that twenty minutes, Mrs. Landcraft had not been killed while trying to treat the scratch—and someone, acting after the fact, had provided an explanation, and so proved the need of explanation. If the bull had been scratched between having his picture taken and killing, the possibility of accident remained—escape remained from the ugliness closing around them.

That escape William Smith, the herdsman, blocked, or almost blocked. He had handled the bull when he was photographed; had guided the photographers, helped them with the animals, while they made many photographs of the barns, of the cattle; had quieted one or two young heifers which were startled by the flashes. (Prince had not been; he was used to photographers; he had nibbled hay.) Smith had led the big bull out into the open area between the rows of stalls, and posed him there, and watched him while he was photographed. When the photographers had finished, he had led Prince back into the stall. Smith had noticed no scratch on the bull's leg when he was handling him, but he had not examined him with any care. He was certain that the bull had not been injured while he was out of his stall.

Smith was a small man with sandy hair and a narrow face. He was very positive.

"And there's nothing in the stall he could hurt himself on," Smith said. "You know that, Mr. Landcraft."

He had spoken to Wade, who had nodded. One does not leave protruding nails, sharp ends of wire, in the stall an international grand champion occupies.

"All I know is," Smith had said, "if this picture shows he wasn't hurt twenty minutes before he went for the old—for Mrs. Landcraft, he wasn't hurt when he did. Before he did, anyway. Because, how could he get hurt?"

For that, no one had had an answer. No one had one now. Smith said he had left the barn, with the photographers, about five minutes before Prince started his bellowing. In those minutes it was conceivable he had been hurt. But, it was only conceivable. It was not really believable.

"Well," Wade said, "do we believe Smith? Because I can't see what he has to gain by lying."

Nobody disagreed.

"We talk as if somebody planned it," Harvey said. "Or, now we do. And we've all been thinking about it. Well, how?" He spoke to his brother. "You know these animals," he said. "Better than I do, anyway. What do you do to make a bull attack somebody? Ballard says he doesn't know. Smith says he doesn't know."

"I don't know," Wade said. "I've thought about it."

Harvey spoke slowly. "Maybe," he said, "it would be a good thing if there wasn't any answer. Because, if there is, it could be murder—as Bonny says. And—when the cops look at murder, they see money." He stopped. Then he stood up and went to the drink tray and mixed himself a drink.

"And we, we four, get the money," Bonita said. "We *are* rather a hollow square, aren't we? Does anybody want to confess?"

Evelyn said, "*Bonny!*"

"We'll be asked," Bonny said. "Don't think we won't. We stand to profit—and who else? Ballard loses a good job. So does Smith—so do the rest of the people around. We get money and—may as well tell them, Harv. In the lodge."

"Got cancelled last week," Harvey said. "I suppose that's what Bonny means. It's not so serious as all that but—"

"But if we stay cancelled, along about spring we're going to need some money," Bonita said. "And we were talking about holding a sale in the spring, weren't we?" She paused. "We may as well look at things," she said. "They're going to be looked at—when Captain Heimrich sees that picture."

And, Evelyn thought—thought heavily—Wade wants to get away from this and I want him to get away, and there'll be so many to guess that. And she was hard to get along with and—

"All the same," Wade said, "we don't suspect one another. I see what you're getting at, Bonny—hell, we all see it. But we don't suspect one another."

"No," Bonny said. "Oh no. *We* don't."

"There were a hundred and fifty people around here," Harvey said. "Anyone of them might—hell, we don't know what somebody *did* do, if anything."

"No," Wade said.

"This man Thayer," Harvey said. "The one who stayed last night—"

"Was going to stay," Wade said. "He left after—after it happened. Why Thayer?"

"I don't know," Harvey said. "Was he a great friend of mother's?"

"Well—" Wade hesitated. "Actually, she didn't like him much. Didn't seem to, anyway. I don't know why she asked him to stay overnight. Probably just being nice to him in the hope he'd buy a lot. Good man to sell to. Got a reputation of buying tops. But—why Arnold Thayer, Harv?"

"He was here. One of the few whose name I got."

Harvey shrugged.

"Any port in a storm," Bonny said, and Harvey said he supposed it came pretty much to that.

"This woman who thought something was the matter with Prince," Harvey said. He still stood by the tray of drinks, but had only sipped from the glass he held. "Is there, by the way?"

"No," Wade told him. "Ballard and the vet agreed he was overweight. Brought him down a little. You mean Florrie Haskins."

"If that was her name," Harvey said. "She a great friend of mother's?"

"So far as I know," Wade said. "They seemed to be. Went to sales together."

"No—animus?"

"Not that I know of."

There was a momentary silence.

"Look," Wade said. "When we come down to it, mother didn't tell me much about–about a lot of things. She thought I wasn't a lot interested and–well, she was right. That's going to come out too, incidentally–if things begin to come out. The way things are, Evvie and I can get away. But what I'm saying is–she probably knew most of the hundred and sixty–it was about that–people who were here last night. Had dealings with a good many of them. Maybe some of them didn't like her. You all know she managed to get her own way when she could and–didn't mind stepping on toes."

"It could be a good deal of trouble for the police," Bonny said. "Maybe–they don't like to go to too much trouble."

"Perhaps they won't go to any," Evelyn said. "Perhaps all this is just because we're worn out, not looking at things straight. Because–look at it–what have we got to go on? We can't–well, to begin with–we can't seem even to guess what we think somebody did. That's the first thing. Bonny talks about–about murder. But–*how*? Even Alec can't guess, or Smitty." She paused. "Perhaps we're just scaring ourselves," she said.

"I whistle a little tune," Bonny said. "Not that you haven't got something, darling." She sat up, suddenly. "You know, maybe she has," Bonny said.

"Maybe," Harvey said, and looked at his brother. Wade was looking at nothing; for some time did not speak.

"If there's a way, the doc would know," he said. "The vet. Doc Nugent. I suppose I could–" He stopped. "We've got to know, haven't we?" he said then, and stood up. He seemed, in silence, to ask the approval of the others.

"It—we'll be the ones to make the point," Harvey said. "We have to realize that."

"It's better to make it," Evelyn said. "Can't you all see? Perhaps we're only seeing ghosts."

"And," Bonny said, "if we're not—we're still the ones ought to make the point, aren't we, Harv?"

So Wade Landcraft went out of the room to the telephone in the office. He was not gone briefly. When he finally returned, Evelyn saw in his face all that she did not want to see, had desperately hoped she would not see.

"Heimrich's guessed a way," Wade said, his voice heavy. "He and Doc Nugent have guessed a way."

Still slowly, his voice still heavy, he told them what the way was.

It meant, Bonita said, in a still voice after a long pause, that if it had been done, it had been done by someone who knew cattle. . . .

When Evelyn left Deep Meadow Farm, drove her light convertible down the long drive to the secondary road, it had been to drive home. The Merritt house was a few miles up the same little-frequented road, and ten minutes would have taken her there. But at the foot of the Landcraft drive she had turned right instead of left on Old Road, and so toward U.S. 6 and a choice between Brewster and Carmel—or, for that matter, Cape Cod and California. It had been as if other hands had turned the wheel.

Wade's mother was dead, perhaps she had been murdered. Dead—murdered! Her mind sought to reject. In the country night, with the car seeming only to whisper on familiar roads, it was unbelievable that there had been murder so—so *close* to her. Murder did not come close; murder stayed decently far away, in the columns of newspapers. It did not draw a circle, a tightening circle, about people like Wade, people like Harvey and Bonita, like herself. One did not listen to inflections in the voices of people so close, draw inferences from things said, from glances, even from silences. One did not uneasily, fearingly, doubt those nearest. (Had Bonita really, in the tone of her voice only said—watch out for yourselves, *we're* all right? In Wade's eyes, once, had there been—?)

She tried to shut her mind to that. If there had been murder, it would not be theirs. There had been—how many people had Wade said? A hundred and sixty?—there had been many people around when Mrs. Landcraft died. The police would find among them—among strangers or casual acquaintances—the one they sought. Or, at the worst, find the sought one among those who worked on the farm—Ballard, William Smith, one of the other men who handled cattle, strung electrified barbed wire to divide the meadows, kept the barns clean. It could not come any closer than that.

She drove through Carmel and beyond, and sought quiet. But her thoughts swirled ever faster. She thought in circles, and after a time a circle seemed to epitomize all things. They were in a narrowing circle; around them in a circle the police were moving, slowly, carefully, with method. The captain, Heimrich, had not seemed like a man who would hurry, or like a man who would tire. She felt suddenly that now he might be anywhere—behind her in a car, waiting for her around the turn ahead, concealed in the forming fog in the valley toward which the little car now descended. She felt that she was, somehow, surrounded by one man—that he surrounded all of them—that—

It was then as if she had been asleep, and had wakened suddenly. She was having preposterous notions. Also, the fog was coming up, as it did so often in the evenings of early autumn. Also, it was getting cooler. She looked at her watch. It was after ten.

She found a place to stop, and put up the top of the convertible. She turned back the way she had come, and realized she should have turned sooner. Fog formed rapidly once it started. Very often, after a few miles, she was dipping the beam of her headlights, slowing the car's speed, for fog patches. They were as often encountered on high land now as in the valleys, which meant that it would, in an hour or so, be everywhere—everywhere, at any rate, where there was water, and there was water almost everywhere around.

It was not as long as an hour. She was south of Carmel, on the winding road, when the patches of fog merged into a veil of fog; when the speed of her car dropped into the twenties, and the beams of her headlights stayed low, seeking the road. Cars coming toward her were now unseen until very close, then seen only as flat lights which seemed to peer, with little hope, from under water. Such cars would hug, as she was hugging, the center line of the road, on which one might guide. Such cars would creep, as she crept. She started her windshield wipers, and they helped a little. It was not really dangerous—if she met only other country drivers—but it was a little exhausting, and very slow. (But now the immediate filled her mind, steadied it.)

The strange thing about it, Evelyn thought, is that, out of a car, this is only a moderate haze. One can walk through fog like this, and see far enough, even at night. One can stand by the side of a road and watch cars grope along it and wonder—although all the time knowing—why drivers made such heavy work of so little. She sighed, continued to make her own heavy work. She almost missed her turn-off when she came to it, although she had taken it hundreds of times.

The fog was not less on the side road, although she had hoped it might be. Sometimes it was. She knew by turns and vaguely seen contours of ground and trees when she crept past the drive to the Landcraft house. She could not see the house itself. She kept to the middle of the road now, and hoped no neighbors would be abroad. Anyway, she thought, if I do run into anybody now, it's almost sure to be somebody I know.

But when she almost did run into a small car stopped on her right, half on road and half on inadequate shoulder, two men were standing behind the car, apparently in conversation, and the taller seemed to have an arm around the shoulders of the shorter. Her headlights picked them up only hazily, as they picked up all other objects. And her mind was instantly occupied—with the need to brake, to swerve, to creep past in space which was just enough. She was too occupied, for the moment, even to resent the stupidity which chose such a place, on such a night, for conversation behind a carelessly parked car.

She got around and then, on the crown of the road again, sounded her horn briefly, chiding. She continued her slow groping way toward home. She had gone only a hundred yards when headlights appeared in the rear vision mirror.

She regretted her horn's angry comment, then. The two men were using her as a guide; probably had been waiting for a guiding car. She slowed even further, so as not to out-run them; so as to give what brief help she could. It could only be a few more yards of help.

She came to her drive, blinked her signal light, and turned in. She half expected the trailing car to follow up the drive, but it did not. When she stopped outside the garage and got out to open the overhead door, the car which had trailed her was not in the drive.

When she was out of the car there was, as she had supposed would be true, hardly any fog at all. She could see the length of the drive, to the road.

And she saw a car stopped there, opposite the entrance to the drive, its lights appearing to cut ahead of it through the fog. They're really lost, she thought, and wondered whether she should go down, on foot, and advise the groping men. But at that moment the car started up, and went ahead on the road.

It went surprisingly fast, with confidence. While she still watched, the driver switched on amber fog lights, which hugged the ground.

She watched the car move away, at first only with surprise. But then she thought, it's as if they had been following me to see where I went, to find out who I was.

She found she was trembling a little as she got back into

the convertible and drove it into the garage. She did not stop the car quite in time, and bumped gently into the back wall of the garage.

Why, Evelyn Merritt thought, I never did that before!

VIII

ABOVE PAWLING, AT a little after nine the next morning, Ray Crowley turned the unidentified sedan off Route 22, onto a side road. Almost at once, in the field on their right, there were black cattle, seemingly afloat in the grass. Half a mile farther along the road, there was a gateway, with a sign beside it—"The Haskins Farm." Under the lettering, there was pictured the head of a black bull. Crowley turned the car into the drive, and it was almost at once surrounded by dogs which appeared to be on stilts. It was evident that they resented the car, would be happy to destroy it, and its occupants. "Breeds wolfhounds," Crowley said, and slowed his speed, sounded his horn at a hound which nonchalantly risked long body and high, spindly legs. The drive branched, a section circling toward a brick house. Crowley took the other.

"Be at the barns this time of day," he said. "Or the kennels. Or where she keeps the cats."

"Cats?" Heimrich said.

"Breeds cats, too," Crowley said. "The ones with blue eyes and funny voices. Siamese?"

They approached barns.

"Used to breed horses," Crowley said. "Gave them up for Angus." He braked, and sounded the horn again. He grinned, suddenly. "Compensation, in a way, maybe," he said. "It's *Miss* Haskins. Always has been, they say."

A man in dungarees came out of the nearest barn and looked at them. He was asked, by Crowley, if Miss Haskins was around. He jerked his head toward the interior of the barn. The dogs leaped around the car and barked at it.

"Come off it, you," the man said, in a voice of command. The dogs stopped and looked at him. There were, after all, only three dogs. Heimrich had estimated a dozen. "You heard me," the man said, to the most attentive dog. "Think they're watch dogs," the man said, to nobody in particular. "Get out of here," he said, to the dogs, who looked at him with reproach. "Out!" he said, with emphasis. The first dog went, in no hurry, to the shade of a tree and lay in it. The remaining dogs looked at the first with interest, appeared suddenly to remember long nurtured plans to lie in shade, and joined their leader. They all put out pink tongues.

The man went back into the barn, and Heimrich and Crowley followed him. The man pointed to a stall, very like the stalls at the Landcraft place, occupied by another large black bull. Florence Haskins was squatting beside the bull, looking at its feet.

"Miss Haskins," Crowley said, and she stood up. She wore dungarees and was compressed by them. She wore what appeared to be an old army shirt. Her very white hair was neatly coiled; her round pink face shone brightly. She looked at the two men through smallish blue eyes. She said, "Oh, it's you. Finish up here, Ben," and came out of the stall. "Want to talk to me, Ray?"

"If you don't mind," Heimrich said, and was looked at. "So you're the one," Florence Haskins said. "All right, come on up to the house."

She walked off, and they walked after her. They went in through the rear of the house, and through a room in which some cats were caged, and others wandered freely. It was a large room. She stopped at a cage and peered in. She said, "Hello, buster," to the occupant, a slender, sleek cat with brown ears and narrow brown face, a *café-au-lait* body. The cat responded in a guttural voice.

"Grand champion," she said. "At stud." Absently, she picked up one of the free-roaming cats, who climbed to her shoulders and draped there. She wore the cat out of the room and along a corridor, into what was evidently an office. She sat behind a desk and the cat remained on her shoulders, so that two pairs of bright blue eyes regarded Captain Heimrich and Trooper Crowley.

"Want a drink?" Florence Haskins said, and opened a desk drawer. Crowley looked abashed; Heimrich said it was a little early for him.

"Been up since five myself," Florence Haskins told them and took out a bottle and a shot glass. She poured the glass full, and emptied it. "Your name's Heimrich," she told Heimrich. "Get down, sweetheart, you're hot." She lifted the cat from her shoulders. The cat sat on the desk and continued to regard Heimrich and Crowley. Heimrich regarded the cat; it was the cat who closed eyes. "What you want is gossip," Miss Haskins said. "You think somebody got the bull to kill Margaret."

"Now Miss Haskins," Heimrich said, "I'm trying to find out."

He was not surprised. He had worked many years in country places. News spread by osmosis.

"Never heard of anything like that," Florence Haskins said. She looked at the bottle thoughtfully. She corked it and put it back in the drawer. "What's your theory?"

Heimrich told her; she appeared to consider it. She nodded. "Doc Nugent ought to know," she said. She stroked the cat absently, and the cat purred.

"She was thinking of firing Ballard," Miss Haskins said, and looked at Heimrich with very bright eyes. "She knew Prince was out of condition, even if Wade didn't. The bull's peaked."

Heimrich closed his eyes, and remembered a bull which had seemed perfect. He said, his eyes still closed, that the bull had looked all right.

"You know anything about bulls?" she asked, and Heimrich shook his head. "So," she said. "Wake up, man."

Heimrich opened his eyes.

"You wanted a motive," she said. "What do you think of that one?"

"Now Miss Haskins," Heimrich said. "Go on."

"She talked it over with me," the bright-eyed woman said. "Said she'd begun to think Ballard didn't know his job. Thought she could get along without him, be her own manager. Ballard's got a nice thing there. House of his own. Good wages. Also, she's let him buy a few pretty good heifers cheap. He wants to start a herd, but he's not ready yet. He needs the job." She stroked the cat. "You want gossip," she said.

"You think," Heimrich said, "that with Mrs. Landcraft

no longer in charge, Ballard will keep his job? That the brothers won't fire him?"

"No," she said, "I don't. But—I think he probably does. Thinks that with Wade in charge, he'll be the one who really runs the farm. Because he's not a cattle man, poor Wade. Nice enough boy, going to marry a pretty girl, but he's no cattle man." She sighed and shook her head. Heimrich found himself sharing her evident feeling that it was too bad about poor Wade, cut off, thus, in his youthful prime.

"What I think," Miss Haskins said, "is that they'll disperse the herd. You read *Variety*?"

It was a long jump. Heimrich did not take it without a stumble. He said, "I'm sorry, Miss Haskins?" and waited.

"Bible of show biz," she said, and Heimrich said, "Oh, I know *Variety*, naturally."

"Harvey's show's been axed," she said. "So, he'll need money. The quick way is to sell the herd. He doesn't even pretend he's a cattle man."

Heimrich had not used all the previous night for sleeping. He had used the telephone. He had learned that Harvey Landcraft was the producer-director of a television show. ("Domestic comedy. Like the Lucy show, or as near as is legal," his informant had told him.) He made a good thing out of it. But—

"Axed?" Heimrich repeated.

"Sponsor's dropped it," Miss Haskins said. "You ought to read *Variety*, captain. Wouldn't miss an issue myself. Of course—" She stopped, because Heimrich had begun to nod at her; because, so, Heimrich indicated that he had remembered.

"You used to be on the stage," he said. "A—few years—"

"*Few!*" she said, and laughed, and her laughter was hearty. The Siamese cat turned and looked at her in reproach, and poured herself to the floor, and went away from there. "A generation, man. Before your time."

"Now Miss Haskins," Heimrich said. "Not entirely. However—"

(She had been slender then; her blue eyes, in a face less plump, had been larger. And one play in which she had been first featured, then starred, had run for almost two years.)

"No business like show business," she quoted now. "Phooey. Dad died and left me this money and you can keep *me* down on the farm, all right. Where was I?"

"You were suggesting," Heimrich told her, "that the Landcrafts will sell the herd, because—I gather—Wade isn't much interested, and Harvey's not interested at all—and needs money."

"You wanted gossip," she said. "Actually, I don't think you've got anything. Because, I think Margaret annoyed the animal and he turned on her." She paused. "Margaret was a great girl," she said. "But she did annoy sometimes. People, anyway. About cattle—" She paused.

"The bull was gentle," Heimrich said. "Everybody agrees to that."

It occurred to him that he had been saying very much that for hours.

"How did Mrs. Landcraft annoy people?" he asked.

"Didn't baby them," Miss Haskins said. "People like to be babied. Call it tact. Margaret, when she thought she was right she went ahead. Thought something was coming to her, went out to get it. Sometimes, I'll give you, her bark was worse than her bite, but how were people going to tell? Take Arnold, now. I'm not saying yes or no, you understand but—"

"Now Miss Haskins," Heimrich said. "Arnold? Arnold Thayer?"

"Only Arnold I know," Florence Haskins said. She paused, however. "In the business, anyway," she said, clearing that up. "How was he to know whether she'd go through with it?"

Heimrich closed his eyes and for seconds said nothing.

"I haven't any idea what you're talking about," he said then. "As you know, naturally."

"It'll be libel, probably," she said. "Or would it be slander?"

Heimrich merely waited, with his eyes closed.

"She told me about it," Florence Haskins said. "Maybe told other people. Arnold's got this bull—Archimedes Two Hundred Thirty-First. Number's part of the name, you know. Or do you?"

"All right, Miss Haskins," Heimrich said. "Go on."

"Showing him at the International this winter," Miss Haskins said. "Been showing him in the western shows and had good luck. Margaret and I were out west and saw him and Margaret said there was a tie, and accused Arnold of fixing it. Said she'd challenge at the International if he showed Archimedes. Whether she would have, nobody'll ever know now. But you can see where it put Arnold."

"No," Heimrich said. "You mean a tie between this animal and—"

"My god," Florrie Haskins said. "What *do* you know, captain?" She looked at the large watch on her wrist, and appeared to find confirmation in its report. She opened the drawer again and removed the bottle and the glass. She said, "Got another glass. Got a couple more."

Heimrich found himself tempted. He resisted. Miss Haskins did not resist. "Doctor's orders," she said, and put the bottle back. "A tie in the back, of course." She appeared to think that all had been made glass-clear. But Heimrich shook his head. Miss Haskins had pity and explained.

There is, Heimrich learned, a tendon in the bovine back which may be too tight, drawing so as to leave a depression, a kind of cup, in a back which—with Angus—should be table-flat. A bull, or steer or heifer, with such a tie has no chance in competition. "Like a Siamese with a kinked tail," Miss Haskins said, again making all clear.

There are two ways to remedy this defect, but both are illegal. The tendon may be cut. The depression in the animal's back may be filled with paraffin, under the skin. "Friend of mine had her nose fixed that way, long time ago," Florence Haskins said. "It spread, though." She paused. "Worst in hot weather, as I remember," she said.

It was a "fix" by the paraffin method which Margaret Landcraft had charged against Arnold Thayer, in relation to the bull Archimedes. The charge, Margaret had told Florrie Haskins, was made privately, and denied with vehemence.

"As a matter of fact," Florrie said, "I think she was seeing things, or feeling them. Bull looked all right to me. Felt all right, too. But, anyway, she told Arnold she was going to challenge."

Heimrich waited, his eyes closed. "Seems like I'm boring you," Florrie Haskins said. "Or were you up all night?"

Heimrich opened his eyes. He said, "Now Miss Haskins, go on please. How would she have challenged?"

It was a method provided by the rules. Any member of the association—the American Aberdeen-Angus Breeders' Association—who suspected such chicanery could challenge publicly, and demand that the suspected animal be killed and examined. If no evidence of tampering was discovered, the challenger was required to pay the value of the animal destroyed. "I've never known a bull challenged," Florrie Haskins said. "They run into a lot of money if you're wrong. But—it could be done, if you wanted to take the chance. At least, by the rules it could. I've known steers challenged."

"If the animal has been fixed?" Heimrich said.

"The breeder gets thrown out of the association," Miss Haskins said. "And that pretty much puts him out of business, of course. Can't show. Can't have a sale under association rules. Can't register his new stock. So, where is he?"

In Limbo, from her tone.

"You think Mrs. Landcraft would have challenged?"

"No, I don't. I think she was sore at Arnold, and wanted to scare him. Not that she didn't think there'd been a fix, or probably had. But I doubt whether she would have gone through with it."

"A bluff, then?"

"Um-m-m—probably. But, if she had gone through with it and had been right—well, Arnold's one of the biggest Angus men in the country. Acts as a judge. Margaret thought—well, that he could be reached as a judge. Had been. That's why she was sore."

"Bribed?"

"Look, man," Florrie said. "*I* don't think any of this. Arnold's all right, for my money. No prize as a man, but an all right breeder. *And* judge, so far as I've ever heard, except from Margaret. And she didn't think it was a bribe, exactly."

"What, exactly?"

Florrie Haskins appeared to consider this.

"An inducement," she said. "Naming no names," she added, with a somewhat unexpected nod to discretion. "There're these people have a big herd and are showing a lot. Suppose a man who might be likely to judge at some shows gets a chance to buy a few good animals dirt cheap? By private treaty sale, you understand. Nobody has to know how much he paid—that maybe he got a ten thousand dollar bull for three or four. See what I mean?"

"Now Miss Haskins," Heimrich said. "Naturally. Mrs. Landcraft suspected that Mr. Thayer had accepted such an—opportunity?"

"Said he had. Said she could prove it. But—" She broke off, and shook her head. "I don't know how she could have," she said. "Also, she didn't do as well in the particular show she was thinking about as she expected to. Not that that would have made any difference to Margaret, according to her—"

Heimrich waited.

"The principle of the thing," Florrie Haskins said. "Margaret was a great one for the principle of the thing. Particularly when it came to doddies. Not that you don't have to be. You see that."

Heimrich thought it over. He shook his head.

"The whole thing rests on people's being honest," Miss Haskins said. "Integrity—Margaret talked a lot about integrity. A bore about it, sometimes. Take Prince, now—his get is worth plenty, of course. Twice as much—more than twice as much maybe—as that of a good run-of-the-herd bull. So, how do I know, if I'm buying, that this yearling *is* Prince's get? I wasn't there. Artificial insemination anyway, nine chances in ten. I've got to take the word of the Landcrafts. Got to be sure they're honest. Don't juggle their records. Mostly, we take it for granted. But Margaret used to make a point of it." She paused. "Made a point of lots of things," she said. "I don't mind saying she could make you pretty damn mad."

She paused, and looked at Heimrich intently.

"Let people talk a lot, don't you?" she asked. "All right, she made me mad a few times. Not enough to set a bull on her, if you're thinking that."

"Now Miss Haskins. I'm not thinking anything in particular—yet. Is falsification of records much of a problem?"

"Don't get the wrong idea, captain," she said. "Cattle people are an honest crowd. Best people in the world. Maybe now and then somebody makes a mistake. Gets records balled up and maybe somebody could come along and—"

She stopped, shook her head.

"Never had any reason to doubt anybody I've traded with," she said. "Not any real reason."

The cat had come back. She raised herself on hind legs

and looked with interest into a waste-paper basket. She decided to get into the basket. She tipped it over. Diligently, then, the little cat, brown ears laid back, began to distribute the contents of the basket. She appeared convinced that, concealed in the bottom, there was a mouse, at least.

"*Ethel!*" Miss Haskins said. "Get *out* of there!"

The cat backed out, looked at Florrie Haskins with interest, went back in again. Miss Haskins pulled the cat named Ethel out by her tail. She righted the basket. It seemed to Heimrich that she made a good deal of doing a good many things. Miss Florence Haskins was a woman of obvious vitality.

She finished with the cat by putting her back on broad, strong shoulders. The cat seemed pleased. Miss Haskins reached up and took the cat down and held her out. "You're not Ethel," she said, accusingly. "You're Lynn." She put the cat back. "Look a lot alike," she said. "Well? Help you any?"

It was, Heimrich decided, dismissal. The cat had interrupted; Miss Haskins had accepted the interruption with—was it really with alacrity? He did not enquire; he thanked the white-haired woman with the bright blue eyes and, with Crowley, went. The three dogs were asleep in the shade; one raised his head, regarded them dreamily, and put his head down again.

The car radio was talking, in a tired voice. "Car one-twenty-nine call in," the radio said. "Car one-twenty-nine call in."

"That's us," Ray Crowley said, and Heimrich picked up

the handset, threw the switch. He identified himself. The voice grew less weary.

There was an item presumably of interest to Captain Heimrich. Joseph Merritt, of Old Road, reported that his daughter, Evelyn, had been followed the night before, or thought she had—been followed home from near the Landcraft farm.

The voice was thanked. The car was headed back to Route 22, through Brewster, onto U.S. 6. At Old Road, Crowley turned right. He passed the entrance to Deep Meadow Farm. It was a little over three miles farther to the Merritt place—a white house in the morning sun, amid neat grounds. They drove up to it, and parked in the drive. A tanned man in tennis shorts and white shirt watched them park from the door of the house. They walked toward him. He had dark red hair; he appeared to be about forty. He said, a little sharply, "Morning, Crowley." He looked at Captain Heimrich.

"Good morning, sir," Crowley said. "This is Captain Heimrich."

"All right," the man said. "What's the idea of following my daughter?"

Obviously, Heimrich thought, not forty. Probably ten years older.

"Now Mr. Merritt," Heimrich said, "we haven't been. Why should we?"

"Precisely," Merritt said. "Why should you? She's a private citizen and—"

"Quit barking, Joe," a much softer voice said, and a pretty woman in shorts and shirt, in a wide gardening hat, came out of the house and looked at them. "Ray," she said.

"How nice. But you shouldn't upset the old man, Ray."

"No, Mrs. Merritt," Ray Crowley said. "We didn't mean to. He—"

The red-haired man laughed, then, and his laughter was as young as his appearance. Heimrich looked from him to the woman who was evidently his wife, presumably Evelyn Merritt's mother. The obvious solution was that Evelyn, instead of being, as he had supposed, in her early twenties, was about ten.

"All right," Joseph Merritt said. "All right. Sorry, captain. Ray. Figured you'd been—" But he broke off. "All right," he said, "who was it, then?"

"He never explains anything," Mrs. Merritt said, and her voice turned the accusation into an expression of approval. "How are they supposed to know what you're talking about, darling? And don't keep them standing there."

They were not kept standing there. Inside, in the room of morning sun, yet cool, they sat. After a time, they talked to Evelyn Merritt. They heard of the men seen in the fog at—Evelyn thought—a little after eleven the night before.

"I thought they followed me," Evelyn said. "But—now I don't know. I was all—tightened up. Driving in the fog and—"

"Damn fool thing to do, Evvie," Merritt said. "When you don't have to."

"I know, Dad," Evelyn said. "—and everything," she went on. "Perhaps I imagined it."

"Saw somebody," Merritt said.

That she did not deny. She had seen two men, one taller than the other, standing by a small car stopped partly on the roadway. "Near the old quarry, Dad," she said. They had appeared to be talking. She thought one man had had his arm around the shoulders of the other—the taller of the two around the shorter's shoulders. The taller man, perhaps both of them, had looked into the headlights of her car, and quickly away again. But she could identify neither.

"It was pretty thick," she said. "I was trying not to run into them."

They had made no signal of any kind. Afterward a car—she assumed the same car, or had then assumed so—followed along behind her, stopped at the juncture of the Merritt drive and the road, then went on, using fog lights after it started up again, and moving faster. She had then, certainly, felt that she had been followed. Now she was less sure.

"I figured it was you people," Merritt said. "Because she's—tied up with the Landcrafts." He nodded at Heimrich. "News gets around," he said. "Didn't see what business you had following Evvie. Scaring the girl." He looked at his daughter. "Not that she scares much," he added.

"Probably all it was," Mrs. Merritt said, "was that these people were trying to find someone—somebody's house. They stopped at our drive and looked at the sign, and we weren't the ones they wanted. Doesn't that explain it?"

She asked the question of everyone. She had removed her wide hat. He smooth hair was dark, save for a white streak near the center.

"That would explain it, naturally," Heimrich said. "One of the men was quite a bit taller than the other, Miss Merritt? And you're sure you didn't recognize either?"

"Yes," she said. "And—no, captain."

"Or the car?"

"No, captain. It was a small car."

"What kind of car were you driving, yourself, Miss Merritt?"

"A Ford convertible."

"You had the top up, naturally."

"Then. After the fog started."

"You'd had it down, earlier? When you were at the Landcrafts'?"

"Yes."

Heimrich nodded. He stood up. He repeated that, if men had in fact followed Miss Merritt, they had not been policemen. He said that, quite probably, Mrs. Merritt's explanation was the correct one. He said that they would, however, look into it further.

Then Merritt asked a question which was obvious. If they accepted the simple explanation, why look further?

"Now Mr. Merritt," Heimrich began, and Evelyn Merritt did not wait.

"Because," she said, and her voice, low now as it had been before, held an odd note of precision—"because you think Mrs. Landcraft was murdered. Isn't that it? That if I was followed, there might be some connection?"

"Yes," Heimrich said. "Naturally, Miss Merritt. I am quite sure Mrs. Landcraft was murdered. But then—you already knew I was, didn't you? Mr. Landcraft—all of you—found that out when he telephoned Dr. Nugent."

"You—" the girl began.

"Oh," Heimrich said. "Dr. Nugent told us, naturally."

"We had to know," the girl said.

"Of course," Heimrich said. "Very understandable. Well—" He moved toward the door. "I wouldn't worry too much about the men who followed you," Heimrich said. "Or seemed to. Mrs. Merritt's probably right—just people looking for a country place."

They went. In the car, Crowley said, "You really think that's all it was, sir? About the men, I mean? Because—"

"You don't," Heimrich said. "Neither do I. I think the two men, whoever they were, didn't recognize Miss Merritt, or her car. There are a good many small convertibles around. I think they wanted to find out who had seen them. They don't know, of course, that she didn't recognize them. If she didn't."

"If she said she didn't—" Ray Crowley began, very rapidly, and then stopped speaking and swung the car around. Heimrich looked at him. After a moment, he said, "Go on, Ray."

He had, Ray Crowley said, spoken out of turn. But—he knew the girl. "I don't think she could lie," he said. Heimrich shook his head at that, said that anybody could lie.

"You know her pretty well?" Heimrich asked.

"Used to," Crowley said. "Oh—pretty well. We went to high school together—anyway, she was there a couple of years when I was finishing. Then she went to a private school. I did have a couple of dates with her—long time ago, now. And—" he stopped. "That's all," he said. "I was out of turn."

"Oh," Heimrich said, "probably she told the truth, Ray. Probably it isn't important, anyway. It's just—a little odd." They were in Old Road again, driving back toward Route 6, toward the Landcrafts'. "I wish she had recognized the men, naturally. Just to—clear up the point. Now, they don't know whether she did or not."

They reached the Landcraft driveway and Crowley slowed the car, looked at Heimrich.

"Yes, Ray," Heimrich said. "It's about time now, I think."

They turned up the drive, parked in front of the house. Ballard did not meet them, this time. They went to the door. Wade Landcraft opened the door before Crowley could press the button beside it.

"Well," Wade Landcraft said, "you got here quick enough."

"Did we?" Heimrich said, mildly. "Well, that's good, Mr. Landcraft."

They went into the house.

IX

WADE LANDCRAFT LED them along the hall, into the library where Heimrich had met them all the day before. There were three men in the room this time; they had been talking, and stopped and looked up. "Oh," Harvey Landcraft said, "hello, captain. Didn't take you long." Ballard stood up, nodded, looked enquiringly at Wade Landcraft. "Better stick around, Alec," Wade said, and Ballard sat down again. The small man, whose face appeared to have shriveled in many suns, merely regarded Heimrich and Crowley, his gray eyes impassive.

"Arnold Thayer," Wade said. "Captain Heimrich. Ray Crowley."

"The attending policemen," Harvey said. Thayer said, "Good morning," in the accents of Missouri.

"You seem," Heimrich said, "to have been expecting us."

"Sure," Wade said. "I just—" He stopped. "I thought it was pretty quick," he said. "I just telephoned. Smith's disappeared."

"Smith?" Heimrich repeated. "Oh—the herdsman? No, I hadn't got any message about Smith. Go on, Mr. Landcraft."

But it was Alec Ballard's story. He had come to the house with it half an hour before.

Smith lived in a small house down the road. "Mile or so beyond the Merritt place." The night before he had not come home for dinner. His wife (Heimrich gathered) had sighed and put the dinner in an oven to stay warm. When he had not come home by ten or so she had (and this, too, was implicit in Ballard's story) sighed again, more resignedly, and taken the dried-up food out of the oven. "Sometimes takes a night off, Smitty does," Ballard said. "Goes over to the Roundhouse. Has himself a few beers. Only takes a few with Smitty."

Mrs. Smith had gone to bed a little after ten. She had slept lightly for some time, expecting her husband. "Waiting to tell him off, you know," Ballard said. But he had not arrived to be told off; his wife had finally gone more deeply to sleep. When she wakened at about six, Smith still was missing. Then she began to worry. At eight, she called on the telephone in the Landcraft barn, and got Ballard, and found that Smith had not showed up for work.

"Supposed to turn up about seven," Ballard said.

Ballard had called "a man he knew" and discovered that the night before had not been one of William Smith's nights at the Roundhouse. He had called elsewhere and made no progress. And when, after several hours, Smith had not appeared, either for work or at home, Ballard had come to the house to report. "Figured Mr. Landcraft would want to know," Ballard said. "With things the way they are. Specially since—" He stopped.

"I tried to get in touch with you," Wade told Heimrich. "Left a message."

"Yes," Heimrich said. "Especially since what, Mr. Ballard?"

"Well," Ballard said, "I don't like to give you any ideas about Smitty, captain. Nice little guy. But—" He looked at Wade, who nodded. "Well," Ballard said, "the old lady—Mrs. Landcraft, I mean—she was going to fire Smitty. Claimed he was stealing. She mention it to you, Mr. Landcraft?"

Wade shook his head.

"Well," Ballard said. "That's what she told me. Nothing much—couple bags of calf starter." He looked at Heimrich. "That's feed for calves. Got a couple of cows on his place, Smitty has, and maybe he was—well, that's what she thought." He paused again. "Smitty was pretty sore," he said. "Wouldn't want to pass on what he said. He's got a temper. You know that, Mr. Landcraft. Nice guy, but he flies off the handle easy."

He stopped. He and the Landcraft brothers looked at Heimrich and waited. Arnold Thayer looked at his fingernails, dissociating himself.

Heimrich closed his eyes. After a moment, he nodded his head. The implications were obvious, of course; his nod acknowledged them. A man with a bad temper; a man with a grudge. It might well be as simple as that. He opened his eyes and Wade said, "Look at this, captain," and handed him a glossy photograph of a black bull. "Prince," Wade said. "Taken night before last. Turn it over, captain."

Heimrich turned it over. He nodded again, looked again at the bull. He said that this was very interesting, and gave the photograph to Crowley.

"You're not surprised," Wade said, and Heimrich said,

"Now Mr. Landcraft. You didn't expect me to be, naturally. But it's interesting, of course. Gives us more to go on."

"Smith was handling the bull," Wade said. "He said—" He told Heimrich what Smith had said. "Of course, he could have been lying."

"Why?" Heimrich asked. "It would have been the wrong lie, wouldn't it? If Smith is the man we want?"

"If he'd decided he couldn't get away with the accident theory," Wade said. "Maybe he—"

Again Heimrich nodded. It was tenable that Smith, having decided that belief was waning in the theory of accident, had elected a part of the truth. But—how did he know that the first plan had failed? Heimrich thought; again he nodded, this time to himself. Smith had led the bull past Heimrich and Crowley the afternoon before; had seen them look at the scratch; might easily have deduced their thoughts. If the accident theory was to perish, Smith might well have thought it would appear most innocent if he were the one to kill it.

"We'll have to find Mr. Smith," Heimrich said. "See what he has to say."

"If you can," Wade said.

Heimrich said he thought they probably could. He sent Crowley out to the car, to get the search started.

"Now," Heimrich said, "there are one or two other points. I—"

"You don't want me here," Thayer said, rather suddenly. He stood up. He was much shorter than the tall brothers. "Think it over," he said. "Let me know tomorrow?"

Thayer started toward the door. For a moment he was

close to Wade Landcraft. The contrast in their height was marked.

"By the way, Mr. Thayer," Heimrich said. "Where were you last night? Around eleven, say?"

Thayer stopped abruptly. He looked up at Heimrich, and his gray eyes were a little narrowed. "*Last* night?" he said. "What about last night?"

"Miss Merritt had an—encounter," Heimrich said. "Nothing of much importance, probably. Met a tall man. And a short man—shorter man. It was her impression that they followed her, for a time. To see where she went."

"You're saying I—" Thayer began. He showed sudden anger.

"Now Mr. Thayer," Heimrich said. "I'm saying nothing, you know."

"I'm average height," Thayer said. He appeared bitter about it. "I—"

"Somebody followed Evvie?" Wade said, and spoke quickly, with insistence. "Skip it, Arnold—you're—*what happened to Evvie?*"

"Nothing," Heimrich said. "She passed a car in the fog. The car was stopped on the road, near an old quarry, she said. After she passed, the car started up behind her. Stopped for a minute at the end of the Merritt drive. Went on. Nothing happened to Miss Merritt, Mr. Landcraft."

"Why?" Wade said. "What did they want?"

Heimrich closed his eyes. He shook his head.

"She couldn't identify them?"

Heimrich hesitated for a second.

"She says not," he said. "If she had identified them we'd ask them what they wanted, naturally." He paused again.

"Her lights were on them for a few seconds," he said. "It was foggy, of course."

"I was nowhere around here," Thayer said. "I was in New York. Took in a movie. What would I be following this girl for?"

"I don't know why anybody would," Heimrich said. "It's possible nobody did. Except by accident, naturally. Happened to be going the same way, on the same road."

"Radio City Music Hall. That's where I was," Thayer said. "Lot of girls dancing in rows. Always go there when I have to be in the big town."

"Yes," Heimrich said. "All right, Mr. Thayer. You didn't happen to be on the road? Either of you?" He spoke to the brothers.

"I was," Harvey said. "With my wife. Is that all right with you?"

"Now Mr. Landcraft. I–"

"Look," Harvey said. "You've set your mind this was murder? We may as well get it in the open."

There was a brief pause. They all looked at Heimrich; all waited.

"Oh yes," Heimrich said. "We may as well get it in the open, as you say. Your mother's death was arranged. I am quite sure of that, Mr. Landcraft."

"Are you," Harvey said, "sure you can prove it?"

Heimrich looked at him. He nodded his head, slowly. He said, "Did you and Mrs. Landcraft happen to stop near this quarry? And–did Mrs. Landcraft happen to be wearing slacks?"

"She was," Harvey said. "We didn't. We drove around

a while, other side of Brewster, got caught in the fog, came home."

"Yes," Heimrich said. "Mr. Ballard?"

"In bed," Ballard said. "Asleep. At the cottage. But I couldn't prove it, I guess."

"I was here," Wade said. "Not asleep. But—what would I want to follow Evvie for?"

"I don't know," Heimrich said. "As I said. I don't know why anyone would. Or that she was. Have you decided what you're going to do with the herd?"

"Who stands to profit," Harvey said. "That's the point, isn't it?"

"Now Mr. Landcraft. One of the points. Well?"

Harvey looked at his brother, and shrugged.

"Probably," Wade said, "we'll have a dispersion sale in the spring. Unless—" He stopped.

"Nope," Arnold Thayer said. "All I want is the big fellow. No tie-in."

"Then it's a general sale in the spring," Wade said. "What you offer doesn't make sense. You know that as well as we do."

"Don't take it then," Thayer said. "You'll go farther and do worse. Ask Ballard. He's your own man."

It occurred to Heimrich that they had, momentarily, almost forgotten him. Of that he approved; it is often convenient to be forgotten.

"There's something in what he says, Mr. Landcraft," Alec Ballard said, slowly. "That's all I say. It's something to think about."

"*Thirty thousand!*" Wade said. "You're both crazy. An international grand—"

"A killer," Thayer said. "Who wants a killer as a herd sire? Don't know why I do."

"Except he's about the best bull in the world."

"Maybe," Thayer said. "Was, maybe. Who wants to handle him now?"

"That's all I say," Alec Ballard said. "You asked me. I don't say it's not pretty much giving him away. All I say is—at an open sale you're taking a chance. Way I see it, you're over a barrel."

"Hell of a chance," Thayer said. "I can tell you that. Tell you something else, if you don't see it." He paused. He shrugged. "What's the point?" he said. "Take it or leave it."

"No," Harvey Landcraft said. "What don't we see, Mr. Thayer?" Wade started to speak. "Wait a minute," Harvey said. "We want to get the picture." Wade shrugged, then.

"O.K.," Arnold Thayer said. "I've been a breeder a long time. Everybody knows that. Knows my herd. I buy Deep Meadow Prince. Looks like I didn't think he's so mean, don't it? People who might think twice about buying his get'll say, 'Old man Thayer don't mind taking a chance. Maybe he knows something.' See what I mean? This gets around you go ahead and have your sale—"

"And it gets around we let a quarter of a million dollars' worth of bull go for thirty thousand," Wade said. "What do we get for the rest of the herd? Nickel apiece?"

Thayer looked at Harvey. He shook his head.

"Sure," Harvey said. "Does Macy's tell Gimble's? Be your age, Wade. Who's to know what he pays? Except—" He looked around the room, then. Heimrich was no longer forgotten. "Hell!" Harvey said.

"Now Mr. Landcraft," Heimrich said. "Nothing illegal's been proposed, as I understand it. The police aren't interested. I'm not." He paused; he closed his eyes. "Directly," he added. "Also, I'm not the Better Business Bureau." He opened his eyes. "I'm interested in murder," he said. "In finding a man named Smith. In a tall man and a shorter man. In—"

"Smith," Thayer said, "is a good deal shorter than I am."

"I hadn't forgotten that," Heimrich said. "By the way—you and Mrs. Landcraft were on good terms, Mr. Thayer?"

Thayer opened his eyes. He appeared to be astonished. So, Heimrich thought, did the Landcrafts and Ballard.

"Me?" Thayer said. "Good terms. Why, sure, captain. Margaret and I were—" He broke off, and his eyes narrowed. "You been talking to Florrie Haskins?"

"Among others," Heimrich said.

Then Thayer laughed, and then the others smiled.

"Good old Florrie," Thayer said. "Contented rattlesnake. Much as a man's reputation is worth to judge one of her Blacks. Unless she wins, and mostly she doesn't. That right, Wade?"

Wade seemed to hesitate. Then he said, "She has that reputation, captain. I like the old girl and—well, anyway, you do hear stories."

Heimrich merely waited. It was his business to hear stories, of various kinds; his habit to wonder who started them; his fate to hear denials. He heard one now, from Thayer. He said, "Now Mr. Thayer, I haven't accused you of anything. Haven't accused anybody."

"But," Harvey said, "you expect to. The people who profit, captain?"

"I try," Heimrich said, "to make the character fit the crime. And—people often help me, Mr. Landcraft. Often by—"

He broke off, as Bonita Landcraft came into the room. She massaged her eyes with delicate finger tips, although her eyes were bright. Just inside the door she said, "Oh, you again, captain," and paused, a hand on the jamb. But then she came on into the room. "Been catching up with my sleep," she said. "Still plugging away, captain?"

"Yes," Heimrich said. "Still plugging away."

"Thata policeman," Bonita Landcraft said. She was immaculate in a dress of pale yellow linen. Her brown legs were bare; green shoes matched the belt of the dress. She was all that a pretty lady from New York should be except —and this Captain Heimrich observed belatedly—quite sober. She had started pre-lunch drinking rather early.

Indications of insobriety had not been obvious, and were not now. It was true that she had, for an instant, steadied herself as she came through the door; it was true that, moving into the room, there had been the faintest possible imprecision in her walk. Yet her eyes were bright; her voice hardly higher in pitch than Heimrich remembered it from the day before. There was more to be inferred from Harvey Landcraft's quick glance at his wife than from anything, since there was so little to put a finger on, that an outsider might have observed unaided. Heimrich had, nevertheless, no doubt that pretty Bonita was a little drunk.

What he did to reveal this knowledge, since he practiced to reveal little inadvertently, he could not have said. But Bonita, swaying not at all (but with the fingers of her right hand pressing a little on a table) looked at him from bright eyes and said, "Shows, doesn't it? The lady is a bum. The lady has drink taken."

"Come off it, Bonny," Harvey said.

Bonita looked at him and smiled pleasantly, and spoke to Heimrich.

"Drowning my sorrow," she said. "Mother-in-law cut off in her prime. My ever-loving mother-in-law. But what can you expect of that-wife-of-Harvey's?"

"Now Mrs. Landcraft," Heimrich said.

"Now Mrs. Landcraft," she repeated. "Now Mrs. Landcraft. Try to be a little lady, Mrs. Landcraft. Remember you're in a house of mourning, Mrs. Landcraft."

She was making it clear enough now. She was, Heimrich thought, doing more than make it clear enough. She was dramatizing it. She was told, by her husband, to be herself and said, "Oh, but darling. I am, aren't I?" with the pleased air of a child. She turned back to Heimrich.

"What it is," she said, "the cork's out. The thumb's off. The cup bubbleth over. Surely—" She stopped, and shook her head. "Not nice to say that," she said. "Not nice at all."

So she sang for a few seconds, instead—in a sweet clear voice; sang, "Shall we dance? shall we dance? shall we dance?"

Then, with entire grace, she sat down, looked around at all of them, and said, "I'm really very sorry, Harvey."

"It's all right," Harvey said. He looked at Heimrich and, for an instant, Heimrich thought he was going to explain something. But he did not—did not even say, although

Heimrich thought it obvious enough—that Bonita had been, and probably still was, under strain, or—

"It's just," Bonita said, "that it's so wonderful—so really wonderful—not to be hated. Not to know that off there, wherever, there's someone hating you, waiting for you to stumble down the stairs and fall on your—break your neck. To make your husband see what kind of woman he's married to while there's still—"

—or, Heimrich finished, to himself, release from strain; from strain too long imposed, too racking.

"It wasn't that way, Bonny," Harvey said. "You—"

"Just imagined it," Bonny finished for him. "I know. Oh, I know, darling. She loved me, didn't she. Oh—oh *darling*. Poor, *poor* darling."

"Skip it, Bonny," Harvey said, and there was much in his voice—a kind of deep anxiety in his voice. "This isn't—"

"Isn't the time," she said. "I know—I do know." She looked around. "I'm sorry, everybody," she said. "It's just —the cork came out." She laughed, and now not happily. "In more ways than one," she said. She put a hand on each arm of her chair and leaned forward. "Nevertheless and notwithstanding, captain," she said, "I did not kill Mother Landcraft. I—I issued no bull. On my honor as—as a no-good little show girl who was ruining—"

And then she put her face in her cupped hands and began, almost soundlessly, to cry. Then Harvey knelt beside her chair and put his arms around her, quite as if no one else were there. He said nothing, but merely held her. Wade Landcraft walked to a window and stood looking out; Alec Ballard and Arnold Thayer did not look away.

But after a few seconds they looked briefly at each other and it was, Heimrich thought, as if they shared something —no doubt, and understandably, embarrassment.

Harvey said something in his wife's ear, and she nodded without removing her hands from her face. They stood up together, and, still with an arm about her, Harvey took his pretty, not entirely sober, girl out of the room.

Wade turned away from the window after the door closed behind them. Heimrich waited.

"She—exaggerates," Wade said, when the silence had begun to be heavy.

"Does she?" Heimrich said.

"She gets excited," Wade said. "It only takes a couple of drinks sometimes."

"Oh yes," Heimrich said. "But—" He waited.

"Mother didn't like her much," Wade said. "That's true. She didn't—couldn't—understand a girl like Bonny. But —she didn't feel the way Bonny said. Not—waiting for Bonny to make a misstep or—" He stopped. "I'm sure she didn't," he said. He did not, Heimrich thought, say it like a man who was sure at all.

There was a long pause.

"I didn't know Mrs. Landcraft was in the theater," Arnold Thayer said. He spoke as if the fact interested him greatly; Heimrich was for a moment surprised, then not surprised, to observe that the little cattle breeder, with a face shriveled like an over-baked potato, moistened his lips with the tip of his tongue.

"As I understand it, Mr. Thayer," Heimrich said, and his voice was as heavy, as without expression, as his face.

"As I understand it, Mrs. Landcraft is not in a burlesque show."

Thayer looked at Heimrich, and at first looked puzzled. But then, just perceptibly, his red neck grew redder.

"Sings and dances on television," Wade said, absently, his mind seemingly elsewhere.

"Oh," Thayer said. "Sure. Well—?"

"Well?" Wade said.

"Offer's open until tomorrow, anyhow," Thayer said. "Another day if you want. Even two."

"All right," Wade said.

"Don't want to rush you," Thayer said. "Talk it over with your brother. Listen to Alec, here. Alec's a man knows the business. And, like your brother says, I'm not a man boasts of making a good deal. Say I paid—hell, man, say anything that doesn't make me look a fool. Hundred thousand if you—"

"All right," Wade said. "I'll talk it over with Harv. Listen to Alec. Only—"

"Sure," Thayer said. "I'll be getting along." He looked at Heimrich, his gray eyes cold. "If it's all right with the officer here?"

"Now Mr. Thayer," Heimrich said. "Perfectly all right. If there should be anything more, I'll get in touch with you, naturally. You're staying here?"

"At the inn, in Carmel," Thayer said. "You do that, officer." He said he would be seeing Alec, but Alec Ballard said he was going back to the barns, if Mr. Landcraft didn't want him right then and—when Wade shook his head—went through the door after the much shorter man.

Wade watched them go; waited until they had had time to leave the house.

"Listen," he said then. "I'm going over to see Evvie. See—well, be sure she's all right."

He, evidently, gave Heimrich time to object.

"Of course," Heimrich said. "Why not, Mr. Landcraft? I'll go look for Mr. Smith."

Wade nodded his head, nodded quickly.

"If mother was—killed," he said. "It looks like Smitty, doesn't it? As if he'd got scared and—run?"

"Why yes," Heimrich said. "It does look like that, Mr. Landcraft."

X

"Yes, Ray," Captain Heimrich said. "It does look like Smith. About to get fired, maybe charged with theft and, they say, got a quick temper. Maybe he had an argument with Mrs. Landcraft and let himself get out of hand and hit her with something. It could be that way, naturally. And then staged the business with the bull. Got scared when we began to look into things and ran. Nice and simple that way. All we've got to do is catch Mr. Smith."

"But—" Ray Crowley said. He was driving them slowly along Old Road, between the Landcraft place and the Merritts'. It was a little after noon.

"Oh," Heimrich said. "I like things simple, Ray. If you can get them that way. Along here somewhere?"

"Little farther on, at a guess. Couple hundred yards this side the Merritts'," Crowley said, and drove a little farther on. He started, then, to turn right onto the shoulder, but was told to wait. They left the car on the road, which it almost blocked, and moved slowly along the shoulder, looking at it.

"Too dry, I'm afraid," Heimrich said. "All right, pull off, Ray."

Ray Crowley got back into the small sedan and guided it onto the shoulder, which was not wide enough for it. Then he joined Captain Heimrich, and pointed.

"Down—" he began, and stopped as a car slowed on the road, went slowly around the police car. It was a Plymouth sedan; Wade Landcraft was driving it. He raised a hand in greeting, and drove on.

"Going to see his girl," Heimrich said. "Didn't have any trouble recognizing us, did he, Ray?"

"It was dark last night," Ray Crowley said. "There was a lot of fog, captain."

That he realized, Heimrich said. He said that, in spite of the fog and darkness, people standing by the road might expect to be recognized, or think it possible.

"You know how it is," Heimrich said. "Fog's always thicker when you're trying to drive through it. Now—this quarry?"

"Down that way," Ray said, and pointed. He pointed to a field of goldenrod, bright in the sun, sloping gently away from the road. Heimrich sneezed, mildly.

"No," he said, "I haven't, Ray. Sympathy for those who have. No sign anybody's been through, is there?"

There was not.

"Well," Heimrich said, "we may as well have a look, now we're here."

They went through an unbroken field of goldenrod; they went for perhaps two hundred yards. They stopped abruptly. The gentle slope became an abrupt declivity. They stood on the verge of a precipice and looked down on sunny water, fifty feet below. At the most distant point of an oval lake, three young men and a girl were swimming. As they watched, the girl went to the end of a low diving board, bounced, and went in and splashed. The young men treaded water, laughed, slapped the water with their hands.

"Very pretty place," Heimrich said.

The quarry had been worked into the side of a hill, so that the rock wall above which Heimrich and Ray Crowley stood became the sheer backdrop of an amphitheater—an amphitheater now deep in sparkling water. As they looked across the water, the bank most distant sloped gently into it, and it was there that the springboard had been rigged and the young men and the girl frolicked.

"It would," Heimrich said, "be an idea to fence this side, wouldn't it? Quite a drop." He pointed; below them rocks jutted from the water. "No happy landing," Heimrich added.

Ray Crowley nodded. He said there never had been a fence, and never any talk of a fence. But he had, he said, never heard of anybody's falling.

"People who live around here know about it," he said. "Nobody else ever finds it, I guess. Hasn't been worked for maybe fifty years. It's always been a swimming pool since I can remember."

"Deep?"

Perhaps twenty feet beneath the cliff; shallower at the other end. Crowley waited.

"Wouldn't be so pretty on a foggy night, would it, Ray? Fog coming up off the water. A gloomy place then, I'd think. A kettle of fog."

"It's pretty enough in midsummer," Ray said. "Get a good moon now and—" He stopped. He grinned at Heimrich. He remembered Heimrich's rank; remembered their business. "You think Smith?" he asked.

Heimrich slightly pursed his lips. Then he said he didn't know. Then he sighed, and said there were so many things they didn't know. He led the way back through the goldenrod to the car.

Behind the wheel, Crowley awaited instruction. None was immediately offered. It was warm in the car, which stood in early afternoon sun. Captain Heimrich closed his eyes, and appeared to have fallen asleep.

"The point, Ray," he said, without opening his eyes, "is that we always get around too late. I do, anyway. What was Mrs. Landcraft like, Ray? Hard to get along with, apparently. Dominating. Not tactful, according to Miss Haskins. Wanted something, went out to get it. Didn't approve of her daughter-in-law. Kept her younger son home on the farm, when he didn't much want to be a breeder, perhaps. Threatened to fire Ballard, Miss Haskins says. And Smith, Ballard says. And to make trouble for Arnold Thayer, Miss Haskins says." He paused. "Says a lot of things, doesn't she? Quite a woman, Miss Haskins," he said. "Mrs. Landcraft bored her about keeping records straight. I wonder why, Ray?"

Ray Crowley said he didn't know. Unless—

"Yes," Heimrich said. "There's that, Ray. But—there are so many things, aren't there? You'd think breeding cattle would be a placid thing, wouldn't you?" He sighed. He opened his eyes.

"Under all that, Ray, what kind of woman was Mrs. Landcraft?"

He appeared to expect an answer. Ray Crowley merely shook his head.

"No," Heimrich said, "we don't know, do we? Heart of gold under rough exterior? Diamond in the rough? Or—rhinestone in the rough? That happens too, you know. Did she really want Bonita to make a slip; want to break up the marriage?"

Ray looked at him.

"The girl seems to think so," Heimrich said. "But the girl was a little drunk, Ray. Saying what she meant because she was? Or more than she meant, because she was? She's very much in love with her husband, apparently. Might go to lengths to keep him. But—did she need to? So we come back to Mrs. Landcraft. What kind of woman was she?" He opened his eyes. "We never meet them till they're dead, Ray," he said. "So we have to put them together from bits and pieces. And—it's what they were we need to know, most times. Characters to fit the crime—but two characters to fit it, Ray." He closed his eyes.

"I guess I don't help you much," Ray Crowley said.

"Oh, I talk a lot," Heimrich said. "Helps straighten things out sometimes. How many would you say we had, Ray? As possibilities?"

"Everybody who was there," Ray Crowley said.

It was a way of looking at it, Heimrich agreed. A very uncomfortable way of looking at it. They might, of course, have to take that way in the end.

"In which case, we'll need luck," Heimrich said. "More than we're apt to have. Because, at a party like that, there's not much point in looking for exclusive opportunity, naturally. People all over the place, going every which way, never looking at watches. Wandering around, going down to look at the bull. Wade and Harvey ran down after they heard the bellowing—they say. Ballard was in another barn when he heard it—he says. So was Smith, apparently. Bonita had gone into the house—to the bathroom. Or, so she says. Thayer had gone up to a guest room to go to sleep—he says. The Merritt girl was sitting on the terrace. No cross check on any of it. All very disorderly."

He sighed again. He seemed, Ray Crowley thought, very disheartened.

"And," Heimrich said, "so many motives. Both the brothers get money. So, indirectly, do the girls. Harvey apparently needs it, if Miss Haskins is right, and probably she is. Because anyone can buy a copy of *Variety,* naturally. Money will let Wade off the farm. But—how badly does he want to get off? And—Miss Merritt won't have to live under a mother-in-law's thumb, will she? How heavy would the thumb have been, d'you suppose? Comes back to Mrs. Landcraft, doesn't it? It all does."

"You've got Smith," Crowley said.

The trouble was, they didn't have Smith. Because he was guilty and had run? Or—

"You see," Heimrich said, "until we find Smith we haven't got anybody. If we don't find him, probably we'll never have. He's all the reasonable doubt anybody needs. There's a murder—or we say there is. A man runs, or seems to run. Anybody else can thumb his nose, naturally."

"The description's out," Crowley said. "We'll pick him up."

"Probably," Heimrich said. "Did Mrs. Landcraft have something on Thayer? And—was she going to use what she had? Or—on Miss Haskins? On Ballard? And—was her bark worse than her bite, or wasn't it? It all comes back to what she was and—" But then he stopped. For some time he said nothing. Then he said, "You know, Ray, perhaps it doesn't. Because—the bull's still alive, isn't he?"

"That's right," Crowley said, in a tone which meant nothing whatever, because the remark meant nothing whatever to Ray Crowley.

"It might come down to that," Heimrich said. "It just might, Ray. Let's drop by the Merritts' again."

They drove up the road, turned in the Merritt drive. This time, Evelyn Merritt and Wade Landcraft were sitting in adjacent lounging chairs, in a shady place near the drive. Heimrich, alone, walked across the lawn toward them, and they looked up—came up, Heimrich thought, out of the depths of conversation. Wade started to get out of the chair, and was asked not to disturb himself. Heimrich would not be a minute; this time there was only a point.

"The men you saw last night, Miss Merritt," Heimrich said. "One of them—the taller—had his arm around the shoulder of the other. You said that?"

"Yes," Evelyn said.

"In a friendly way?"

"Why—yes, I suppose so."

"And—you're still quite sure you didn't recognize the men? Or—either of the men?"

She nodded her head. "Quite sure," she said. "If I had, why wouldn't I tell you?"

"Now Miss Merritt," Heimrich said. "I don't know, naturally. I'd think you would. Unless—" He stopped. He waited.

"I was protecting someone?" Evelyn said. "Is that what you mean? But—from what, captain? They—they weren't doing anything."

"No," Heimrich said. "Apparently not. At least—" He broke off. "Or," he said, "unless, you wanted to be sure before you said anything. Ask somebody you thought it might have been. Give somebody a chance before—well, before you told us."

"No," she said, and at almost the same time Wade Landcraft did get up out of the chair, so that he faced Heimrich. He was a little truculent. He demanded to know what Heimrich was getting at, thought he was getting at.

"Oh," Heimrich said, "murder, Mr. Landcraft. What did you think?"

And, without waiting for an answer, Heimrich turned and walked back to the car. He was a very solid man, viewed as they viewed him. He seemed to walk with great certainty, in the straightest of lines. Why, Evelyn thought, he'd walk over anything that got in the way. She found she was, suddenly, rather chilly.

"Personally," Wade Landcraft said, "I don't think he's getting anywhere. Nowhere at all."

She did not answer him.

In the car, Crowley waited.

"I'm afraid," Heimrich said, "we're going to have to drag that quarry of yours. Unless it can be drained somehow?" Crowley was surprised to hear the captain speak so loudly.

"I don't think there's any way to drain it," Crowley said. "You think Smith's there?"

They rolled down the drive.

"No," Heimrich said. "But—it's a place to start, isn't it, Ray?"

For a man professedly so sceptical of results, Captain Heimrich became a man inordinately (it seemed to Ray Crowley) in a hurry to get them. It somewhat confused the trooper, who had thought Heimrich a policeman marked by patience—by patience, and doggedness. But now, in the matter of dragging a pool in which he apparently did not much hope to find anything, Heimrich became a man who could not wait. One would have thought that, if in the pool, William Smith might at any moment rise out of it and walk away.

To township and county officials, with whom Heimrich talked first from the car radio, afterward by telephone, still later in person, the great need to rush the matter forward did not appear. If Heimrich wanted the quarry pool dragged, it would be arranged, although, patently, dragging was felt to be a nuisance. If he insisted, it might be done the next day; the day after at the latest. "Now," Heimrich said, and as time went on said it with the air of a man who might, at any moment, go to the governor about it. "This afternoon."

He was reasoned with. Equipment would be required. Boats would be required. When it came to that, they would want to find a diver, if they were really going to do a job.

"I can do that," Crowley said, feeling it was time he could do something. "Use goggles and flippers."

He was looked at without enthusiasm, as one who throws a monkey wrench. Heimrich, however, was pleased. Heimrich told him to go get his stuff, as if all now were settled.

"Tomorrow morning," the county man said. "This afternoon," Heimrich told him. "While it's still light." He was told he talked as if it were a matter of life and death; he was asked to consider the fact that, if William Smith were at the bottom of the quarry pool, a few more hours there would not further damage him. Everyone was entirely reasonable with Captain Heimrich. Heimrich was reasonable with no one.

In the middle of the afternoon, a truck provided by the State Highway Department, and a second truck wrested from the Town of Southeast, trundled into Old Road from Route 6. Each truck brought a boat, and grappling equipment, and men. State troopers arrived. Six medium-sized boys, who had replaced the young men and the girl, were plucked from the water—and remained on its edge, fluttering with excitement.

The trucks beat an uneasy way from the road to the shallow end of the pool; men hauled boats from them and set boats afloat. The scene was one of great activity; Old Road, a few hundred yards west of the Merritt house—where an unused trail made access to the pool just possible—was almost blocked by cars and police motorcycles. After half an hour, residents of the neighborhood formed small, observant groups. The medium-sized boys were particularly pleased with Ray Crowley, in trunks, wearing goggles, with rubber webbing on his feet, who dived here and there to peer through clear water, under rocks. Each time Ray emerged from a dive, he was generally applauded.

But Captain Heimrich, who had started all this, was not among the observers. He saw it begun. Then he took the little sedan along Old Road, past the Merritt place, past—within half a mile—two other large places. After that, Old Road, not at its most vigorous a traffic artery, became the least distinguished of capillaries. The pavement worsened; in the end the black top dwindled altogether and the road became merely what is euphemistically called "hard surfaced." It occurred to Heimrich, as he bumped on slowly, that it was hard in the wrong places. The New York State Gas and Electric Company had here, Heimrich noted, abandoned its contribution to rural electrification. Only the poles set up by the New York Telephone Company marched doggedly into this wilderness.

But it was pleasant country. The houses, if small, were neatly white; the fields they stood among, if rolling and rocky, were for the most part cared for. But the mailboxes, like the houses, had grown smaller. They were no longer adequate for parcels posted from Bonwits and Saks Fifth Avenue. He looked for a box marked with the name of William Smith. After he had gone for almost two miles beyond the Merritt place, he began to think that he must have missed it. But he remembered that the term "mile or so," as used by country people, can be elastic.

He was nearer three miles beyond the Merritt place when he found the box, which was on the right of the road, which bore the name he wanted in amateur lettering. But there did not, at first glance, appear to be a house to go with it. The next house, only fifty yards or so farther on the road, had its own box—"J. C. Hendrix." On the opposite side of the road, there was only a corn field.

But a lane led in beside the Smith mailbox and, a little doubtfully, Heimrich put the car into it. It was two tracks, with weeds between—weeds which had swept the bottom of a car and been darkened by oil and grease. The two tracks led between parallel strands of barbed wire, supported on metal stakes. The lane went up a rise; weeds swished under the police car. Heimrich reached the top of the rise and went down it, reflecting that Smith had, evidently, a permanent right of way through land which fronted on the road. He went into a shallow valley and up another rise, wondering what happened when two cars needed, on this lane, to get past each other. He assumed they did not.

A house came into view from the top of the second rise —a small, square house, painted white. At first, Heimrich saw no sign of any life; then he saw a solitary chicken, reddish in color, which was pecking in front of the house. The chicken paid no attention to the car or to Heimrich, who stopped the sedan and got out of it and went to the door of the little house—a door which opened on a low platform, in lieu of porch. His steps were noisy on the platform, and his knuckles on the door. Nothing happened. He walked around the house and knocked on the back door. He tried the knob of the back door, then, and the door opened. He was unsurprised by this; doors of small country houses are seldom scrupulously locked.

He was in a kitchen, small and square and clean, with a kitchen range which used bottled gas. The refrigerator also used gas. But there was an electric ceiling fixture, with a pull cord. There was a table and on the table, held down under a salt cellar, a note. Heimrich read it:

"Dear Bill, Gone to stay with Myrtle. You can find me

there. If you want to." It was signed, "Grace." Heimrich thought it rather touching.

He went through the other three rooms of the house, and went down into the basement, where there was a coal furnace. He went back out of the clean, empty house and into the yard behind it. The reddish chicken came around the house, and now it looked at him. There was a vegetable garden on the right, with broccoli still growing in it. But the broccoli shoots were breaking into yellow flowers. The flowers were pretty enough, yet added desolation—it had been a couple of days, or more, since anyone had bothered to cut the broccoli. There was corn growing beyond the other vegetables, and there were a few ears on it, but they were, Heimrich thought, over-due for picking.

And then he heard a gasoline motor running, its sound muffled. He followed the sound down a path, around cultivated blueberry bushes, and came on a square low structure of concrete blocks, which had somewhat the appearance of a tomb. The sound came from the concrete tomb, and Heimrich went to it. There was a low door, up to which the path led. Behind the structure, on the surface but blocked for permanence, was a large tank. The motor inside continued to put-put contentedly.

The hasp which could secure the door was open; from the staple over which it could be passed dangled an open padlock. Heimrich opened the door of what was obviously a pump house, and looked in. He pulled a dangling cord just inside the door, and a bulb lighted dimly.

It was a pump house, as he had supposed. It was more than that. Along with the pump, the structure housed a small generator, driven by the gasoline motor. It was all neat, efficient, compact. If William Smith had been a larger man there would hardly have been room for him to lie on the cement floor, between the brisk little motor and the pump housing. As it was, he was doubled around the pump.

Heimrich backed out of William Smith's mechanized tomb, and took a deep breath of cleaner air, and held his breath as he went in to shut off the gasoline motor. There was no window in the structure, and the carbon monoxide would dissipate only slowly through the open door. Heimrich came out again, waited, and went back. He had no doubt that Smith was dead. He made sure. Smith had been dead for a number of hours. From the odor of alcohol on the body, he had died drunk.

And it was obvious, after a few minutes of investigation, that Smith had killed himself. A rubber hose had run from the exhaust of the motor through a hole in the side of the pump house. The hose was there, still fixed to the exhaust. The hole was there; it had been chiseled out neatly enough. But the hose did not run through the hole; the hose ran from the exhaust to a place on the floor near Smith's face. It was all quite obvious.

Smith had killed Mrs. Landcraft, possibly in a moment of ungovernable rage. (He had been a man to "fly off the handle.") He had been, subsequently, overcome by remorse, or by fear, or by both. He had come home and gone into the pump house, where the little motor ran, turning the generator, providing the current the New York State Gas and Electric Company had felt it impracticable to furnish. He had closed the door after him, and pulled the hose from the hole he had on some brighter day chiseled through the wall, and put it down on the floor, and lain down beside it, and waited—probably not long—to die. It was all very obvious, very neat. The physical facts told a story which could not be questioned.

And Captain Heimrich of the New York State Police did not, for a moment, believe a word of it.

Leaving the motor off, he went out of the pump house and walked around it, looking for a mistake. He found none—he found a five-hundred gallon tank with a lead-in, automatically controlled, to the smaller tank of the motor itself. He knocked on the side of the tank with a stone, and decided that it was about half full. He looked for other footprints than his own, and found none—the earth was dry, packed. He stood in front of the tomb-like structure and looked at the wooden door which closed it. He could not see that the killer of William Smith had made any mistakes at all. It was a pity, but one had now and then to expect such awkward efficiency.

No doubt, when the body was examined, it would be discovered that Smith had been drinking rather heavily before he died. And that would prove nothing—nothing helpful. He had drunk to nerve himself to die; to swaddle death. Even if he had had a companion in his drinking—someone to say, "Have another, Bill," or, "Take one for the road, Smitty,"—there would be no onus attaching to such encouragement. A man is supposed to know what he can drink.

Heimrich sighed, in the quiet of the warm afternoon. It was all rather unfortunate; it would have been convenient if things had been otherwise.

He crouched in front of the hasp and examined it. It

was rough iron, would retain no useful prints. The padlock might.

Heimrich put the hasp over the staple; handling it carefully, he put the padlock through the staple, and pressed the tongue down into the socket, until it clicked. He tried it, and the lock held. He walked back to the car, opened the trunk, and took out the slender steel rod used to operate the jack. He returned to the pump house, worked the rod into the staple and prized. The staple came loose without too much effort, and Heimrich regarded his handiwork. There was no reason it should not look authentic, since in fact it was. The pump house had been forced open.

It was quite unscrupulous of him, Heimrich thought—or would be, if carried far enough. But it is quite unscrupulous to murder a man and make it appear suicide. It is especially unscrupulous to do this without making mistakes from which the police may benefit.

Captain Heimrich went back to the empty house, looked at the note which would never be read by the man it was meant for, and found the telephone, pleased with the enterprise of the New York Telephone Company, which came back-lots when needed. He got the operator; he got the people he wanted, reported what he needed to report.

"No," he said, "I'll not wait, I think. Got people to see." He listened. "Yes," he agreed, "it was a waste of time. I realize that, naturally."

He drove back along Old Road toward the quarry. He was again on the black-top surface when sirens began to sound ahead. He drove far to the right, to give passing room to the motorcycle men, the patrol car, summoned by radio from the quarry pool, where they had been "wasting time."

As he approached the Merritt driveway he slowed, but then he shook his head and drove on. If Evelyn Merritt had gone to the Landcrafts', it would be inconvenient, but a problem to be met when it arose. Problems ought, from now on, to arise with frequency. Well, Heimrich thought, that's what policemen are for.

At the quarry pool, men were already loading equipment on the trucks, hauling the boats out of the water. The foreman regarded Heimrich dourly; said that they had sure gone to a lot of trouble for nothing.

"It's the sort of thing that happens," Heimrich told him, and picked up Ray Crowley, who no longer was web-footed, and Crowley drove them on.

"We drew quite an audience," Heimrich said. "Most of the neighborhood, wouldn't you think?"

"Well," Crowley said, "we had to expect that, captain."

"Naturally, Ray," Heimrich said.

XI

When Heimrich knocked on the screen of the open front door at the Landcraft house, Harvey Landcraft came through the house from the terrace and let him in. He looked at Heimrich. He said, "I hear you found Smith."

"Yes," Heimrich said.

"Dead?"

"Oh yes," Heimrich said. "He's dead, Mr. Landcraft. Your brother around? Mr. Ballard?"

They were down at the barns, Harvey said. He led Heimrich and Crowley through the house to the terrace beyond. Bonita was there; she and her husband had evidently been sitting side by side when Heimrich knocked. She said, "Oh, it's you again, captain." She appeared now to be entirely sober. She was not, evidently, pleased to see Heimrich. People often were not, Heimrich reflected, and Harvey Landcraft said, "I'll call down—no, here they come now."

Ballard and Wade Landcraft had come through the door of the nearest barn, were walking up the slope toward the house, talking as they walked. They were much of a height, Heimrich noticed—of a considerable height. Ballard was bare-headed; Wade wore a battered felt hat, its brim an irregular undulation.

"Why," Bonita said abstractedly, "does he wear that thing?" It appeared that she was talking to herself.

The two men saw Heimrich and walked faster, across the grass, the late sun slanting behind them.

"Thought you'd show up," Wade said, when they were a few feet away. "So—Smith's found?"

"Dead," Harvey answered for Heimrich.

"The poor little guy," Ballard said. "You'd think—"

They waited, but Ballard did not say what one would think. He shook his head, instead.

"Not in the quarry," Wade said. "You wasted time on that." He said, then, that they might all as well sit down. They did; the Landcrafts and Ballard waited.

"In his pump house," Heimrich said. "You know the place?"

"Sure," Ballard said, and Wade nodded. Harvey shook his head, and Bonita looked out over the green fields, toward the green hills, and said nothing.

"The motor was running," Heimrich said. "I suppose it ran most of the time?"

"He could cut it off," Ballard said. "Turn it on when he wanted power. Cut it off when they went to bed, probably. Started it up in the morning. Ice box uses gas, I know. After he got it set up, he said he didn't care if they ever got the electric from the company. Said this cost a lot less and—" He stopped. "Poor little guy," he said.

"He killed himself?" Wade asked.

"He had a rubber hose to take care of the exhaust," Heimrich said. "Went out through a hole in the blocks.

It had been pulled inside. The place was pretty much air-tight—near enough, anyway."

There was a pause. Then Harvey said that he supposed it was an easy way to do it—as easy as any.

"Oh yes," Heimrich said. "I suppose he just went to sleep."

"Could you tell when it happened?" Wade asked, and Heimrich said that, at a guess, Smith had died some time the night before. He waited, looking around at the three men, at Bonita Landcraft.

"Well," Wade said, "that seems to be that."

"Does it?" Heimrich said.

Their expressions changed, then—all but Bonita's. Bonita continued to look at the hills.

"That Smith killed Mrs. Landcraft, you mean," Heimrich said. "Decided we'd catch him and killed himself. That's what you meant, Mr. Landcraft."

Wade nodded his head.

"Look, mister," Ballard said, "what else would it be? You say Smitty killed himself, so sure we think—"

"No," Heimrich said. "I didn't say Smith killed himself, Mr. Ballard. I said he's dead. Dead of carbon monoxide poisoning, which is a frequent method of suicide. Because, as you said, Mr. Landcraft, it's an easy way. It was meant to look like suicide, naturally. But—Smith was murdered. Somebody knocked him unconscious. Put him in with the generator and pulled out the exhaust tube and closed the door and—waited."

He paused as if for comment; there was none.

"Closed the door," Heimrich said, "and—made his mistake. Very foolish mistake. Perhaps it was an accident, something he—or she, of course—did without thinking. You see—the door was locked when I was there this afternoon. Locked from the outside. I had to force the lock." He closed his eyes. "Padlock," he said. "Through a staple. Couldn't have been done from inside, naturally." He opened his eyes then, and looked from face to face. He saw only surprise; then, on the faces of Wade and Alec Ballard, what he took to be incredulity.

"Look," Ballard said, "nobody would be that much of a damn fool, mister."

"Apparently," Heimrich said, "somebody was, Mr. Ballard. Of course, as you say, it gave the whole thing away. If somebody'd wanted to advertise it as murder, he couldn't have done more."

"Wait a minute," Wade said. "Suppose somebody—Mrs. Smith, maybe, saw the latch open and locked it? Not knowing Smith was inside."

"And," Heimrich said, "without looking? When he was missing?"

"Sometimes," Bonita said, without taking her gaze from the hills, "sometimes people do things without thinking."

"Yes," Heimrich said. "Somebody did, Mrs. Landcraft. But I don't think it was Mrs. Smith. I think that, if she went there at all, she saw the door locked and decided—very logically—that her husband couldn't be there. We'll ask her, but I'd imagine that happened."

Harvey Landcraft spoke slowly. He said that Heimrich was guessing, had to be guessing. He said that, so far as he could see Bonny's guess might be as good as Heimrich's. If the murderer—assuming there was a murderer—had locked the door to the pump house, he must have done it without thinking, as a kind of reflex. But, if you assumed he might do that, you could also assume that Mrs. Smith might, as easily, have done the same.

Heimrich listened, he nodded his head, he said he saw the point, naturally.

"But," he said, "if Mrs. Smith did, why didn't she unlock it again and look in?"

"Didn't think of it," Ballard said. "Or—maybe Smith had the only key on him. Did you think of that, mister?"

"Now Mr. Ballard," Heimrich said. "Yes, I did. I thought of several things. If he had the key, the boys will find it. But I'd think there'd be another key, wouldn't you? That Mrs. Smith could put her hands on, anyway?"

"A very absent-minded murderer," Bonita Landcraft said. "Can't you do better, captain?"

"Now Mrs. Landcraft," Heimrich said. "I can think of alternatives. The murderer locked the door so that Mrs. Smith wouldn't look there for her husband. Meant to go back later and open it again. Or, he locked it so that Smith wouldn't come to and get out. Perhaps there was some reason the murderer couldn't wait around. Had to be somewhere else, perhaps. Again, meant to go back and didn't—or thought there was no hurry, that we wouldn't look there. It doesn't matter too much, does it? One way or another way. The same mistake."

"You had to break the lock to get in?" Ballard asked.

"The staple," Heimrich said. "I pried out the staple."

There was a somewhat long pause.

"I suppose," Harvey said, "you think Smith knew something about—about what you say is mother's murder. Had to be got rid of?"

"Possibly," Heimrich said. "And—possibly it was even simpler. We're looking for a murderer. We are given one—dead. And, as one of you said, that seems to be that. We stop bothering people. Pack up and go home."

"Just like that?" Bonita said. "Without even—hatred? Even dislike?" She looked at Heimrich now. "Because it was useful for him to be dead?"

"Possibly," Heimrich said. "Yes, I think it may have been that, Mrs. Landcraft. A matter of—evaluation. A murderer may have a scale of values it is difficult to understand." He closed his eyes. "We caught a man once who'd killed a woman," he said. "Didn't deny it. Didn't seem to be sorry about it. Completely calm—until we suggested he'd stolen the revolver he killed her with. Very upset by that; kept saying he wasn't a thief." He opened his eyes. "Turned out he wasn't, as a matter of fact," he said. "We had to admit that. He seemed to feel that that cleared everything up."

"It's not the same," she said.

"Near enough," Heimrich told her. "Values upside down. A man up in Canada killed a lot of people in a plane, with a time bomb. Didn't like his wife who was on the plane. Here it could come closer home. Kill Smith, save your own life. You might think it was merely self-defense."

"I?" she said. "Not I, captain." She returned to her study of the distant hills. "If I hated enough—I don't know. But it would be personal. I'd think it would be with—anyone."

"The 'you' was impersonal," Heimrich said. "Like Smith's murder."

"Listen," Harvey Landcraft said. "This is all very well.

Very illuminating, perhaps. But—you don't know anything, do you? It's all speculation."

"Your mother was murdered," Heimrich said. "Smith was murdered, as a result. We know those things. Somebody thought it to his advantage to kill twice."

"One of us, you mean," Wade said. "Harvey or me. For the—advantage."

He hadn't, Heimrich pointed out, said that.

"Yet," Harvey said.

"If you like," Heimrich said.

"For a man who spent hours dragging an empty swimming hole," Harvey said, "you're confident, captain. You could be wrong again."

"Oh," Heimrich said, "naturally. The pool seemed most likely. Because—" He hesitated. "Because I think Smith was to have been thrown into the pool," he said. "From the lip of the cliff, probably. So that any head injuries would be covered up. But—Miss Merritt happened along and saw Smith and the man who was planning to murder him. Even if she didn't recognize the men—she still says she doesn't—the murderer couldn't know that. She'd seen enough so that the quarry plan had to be abandoned. But —not enough so that the whole plan had to be. When she—if she identifies the taller of the two men, he can say he was merely taking Smith home; doesn't know what happened after Smith got home. If we believed in Smith's suicide, that would be that."

"You started," Wade said, "to say 'when' Evelyn identifies the men. She didn't recognize them. You know that."

"Now Mr. Landcraft," Heimrich said. "I've been told that."

"She's not a liar. If she were, why should she lie? You don't argue she's involved herself?"

"Not if she saw two men, as she says," Heimrich said. "Not directly. But—" He stopped. He shrugged. "Of course, she may not have seen anyone."

"You think she did?" Bonita said. "Because—I do. Wade's right, of course. Evvie's not a liar. Most people are, more or less. She's not."

"If she'd recognized the men, she'd have said so," Wade said. He took off the battered felt hat and tossed it to a chair. It was, Heimrich thought, as if he found some physical action essential. "You know damn well she would. Why wouldn't she?"

"Now Mr. Landcraft," Heimrich said, "you know her better than I do. And I can think of reasons. However—" He stood up. "We'll be getting along, Crowley," he said. He started through the house toward the front door.

"You'll be back, I'm sure," Harvey Landcraft said.

"Yes," Heimrich agreed. "We'll be back, I expect."

In the car, Heimrich said, "Carmel, Ray," and then did not speak again until they had left Old Road behind and were on Route 6. Then he said, in the tone of one who notes an abstraction, that it is always annoying to have to let a lie pass, knowing it a lie.

"Which one's lying?" Ray asked him, and Heimrich said he could not prove anything—yet. But he had not, he said, been thinking precisely of that.

"Somebody," Heimrich said, "and I'd think one of the men at least, knows *I'm* lying, Ray. Took it pretty well too, considering. But it must have annoyed him a good deal."

Ray Crowley took his eyes from the road long enough to look at Heimrich, and then went back to his job.

"We can't prove Smith was killed, Ray," Heimrich said, and told him why.

"You could—" Ray began, but Heimrich shook his head. "Not in court, Ray," he said. "We have to draw the line somewhere." He paused. "I suppose," he said, with regret. "But I don't like murderers." He sighed. Then he brightened. "But," he said, "with any luck it won't go that far. Not in that way, anyhow. Let's see what the boys have got in Carmel, shall we?"

* * *

"He's bluffing," Harvey told the others. "Trying to throw a scare into—somebody. Because, there's no way he can know one of the men Evvie saw was Smith. And if it wasn't Smith, it doesn't matter who the other man was. There's nothing he can prove."

"Dear Harvey," Bonita said. "He dragged the pool."

"On a chance," Harvey said. "Or—" He paused. "Under the circumstances, he has to do something. If only for the looks of the thing."

"I don't know," Bonita said, and looked away from the hills, looked around at the three tall men. "It doesn't seem right, somehow. Not for him. If he—if he fiddles while Rome burns, it's to get somebody to dance. To the tune he picks."

"Hell," Harvey said. "He's just a big, slow-footed cop. Furthermore, he tells everything he knows. He's—he's transparent, Bonny. You give him too much. His bluff's transparent."

"He dragged the quarry," she said. "It took time, and

men. Probably it cost money. He knows one of the men was Smith."

"How?" Wade said. "Evvie didn't."

"She says she didn't," Bonny said. "Anyway, she told you she didn't."

She was told that she, herself, had agreed Evvie didn't lie, and she said, "Oh, that." She said, "All for one and one for all." She said, "Perhaps she's told the captain. He's persuaded her not to admit anything to anybody else—even you, Wade."

"Or perhaps," Alec Ballard said, "she did spot Smitty and not whoever was with him. Or—maybe she did spot this other guy and's protecting him."

He did not look at Wade Landcraft; although Wade looked at him, and looked intently.

"Whatever way it is," Bonita said, and turned back to the hills, "he's sure the smaller man was Smith. His dragging the quarry proves that. And so the other man killed Smith. So what he's got to do, is to get the other man identified." She paused. "I hope," she said, "that it's nobody any of us knows."

* * *

It boiled down, Ray Crowley said, to one of two men. Or, stretching a point, they could call it three. For both jobs. He braked the car for a stop sign.

"Now Ray," Heimrich said. "For Smith, probably. Although at the moment we can't prove it. For both jobs? It could be another way. It didn't need a man to kill Mrs. Landcraft. Smith—probably. If he was got drunk and lugged around a good deal. But anybody with any strength at all could have hit Mrs. Landcraft with something, either just outside the bull's pen or, for that matter, inside it. If she was outside, it wasn't far to drag her."

Crowley started the car. He turned right on the main street of Carmel. He said, "The man with Smith?"

"Smith may have seen Mrs. Landcraft killed," Heimrich said. "Somebody else may have decided to help out."

"Two in it?" Crowley said, and stopped the car near the county court house.

He was told that it happened; that it often happened. Conspiracy to murder, the conspirators most often two; conspiracy to save the murderer.

"For example," he said, "if Bonita killed her mother-in-law, her husband probably would help her. If Miss Merritt did, I'd think Wade would help, wouldn't you, Ray? To the point of disposing of Smith, even. If there wasn't another way."

"I can't," Ray said, "see how you can figure Evvie—Miss Merritt, in."

"Can't?" Heimrich said. "Or don't want to? You're not in high school now, Ray."

Ray Crowley flushed.

"Nothing you can help, naturally," Heimrich said. "Let's see what the boys have got for us."

The "boys"—in the person of a county detective, who was in his sixties—had odds and ends. Smith had died drunk, as Heimrich had supposed. Harvey Landcraft's present television show would go off the air in twelve weeks, unless a new sponsor picked it up. So far as anyone knew, it was his only source of income. He and his wife had probably lived up to the income. Friends of Wade Landcraft were of the belief that he might do a good deal to get out of cattle breeding—"fed to the teeth with it," one said. They were also sceptical of, even indignant at, any implied suggestion that, to get out of it, he might have killed his mother. He wasn't "that kind of a guy."

"They never are, of course," Heimrich said, and the county detective agreed they never were, to their friends.

Deep Meadow ran about two hundred head of cattle. There was no way to do more than guess the value of the herd. Before the big bull killed, the herd—excepting its herd bull—might conceivably have sold for half a million dollars; Deep Meadow Prince might himself have brought almost any sum. One international grand champion was reported to have been sold for two hundred thousand. "Some breeders doubt that, though," the county detective said. If Deep Meadow Prince died before he was ten, Lloyd's paid eighty thousand.

Alec Ballard had been a cattle man since he was a boy; had come east from a big breeding farm in Iowa, where he had been herdsman; had been five years at Deep Meadow. He had a small breeding farm of his own, adjacent to the Landcraft farm. He had acquired a few heifers from the Deep Meadow Herd; one or two from Florence Haskins' Rocking River Herd. He had, presumably, got them cheap; they were therefore not, presumably, likely to win many prizes. "His bull's an Angus," the county detective said. "Apparently that's about all." Nobody had heard any rumors that Mrs. Landcraft had been dissatisfied with Ballard—nobody but Miss Haskins. "Quite a girl, Florrie," the county detective said. "Doesn't like Ballard."

The Haskins herd was somewhat larger than that at Deep Meadow. It was generally considered a good herd, but with no outstanding animals. Miss Haskins had, before Prince went international grand champion, offered to buy a half interest in him. Margaret Landcraft had not been interested. Ballard had advised his employer against selling.

"Make Miss Haskins mad?" Heimrich asked, and was told there was nothing to show it. The two women were a good deal together. The incident probably had not made her fonder of Ballard.

"She's well thought of by other breeders?" Heimrich asked. "No suggestion, say, that her records aren't reliable?"

"No," the detective said. "Nothing against her. You think there would be?"

"Now Henry," Heimrich said, "you know how it is."

Bonita Landcraft—then Bonita Carroll—had been a show girl when Harvey met her. She had got into television, first as a dancer, then had sung an occasional song, now and then read a line or two. She had worked in a show Landcraft was directing. They had got married. "Tried it out first, apparently," the detective said. "Lots do, nowadays."

"Yes," Heimrich said. "She wasn't popular with her mother-in-law. That might be one reason."

"Might," the county detective admitted. "Not modern, the old lady wasn't." He paused. "Not myself," he added. "However, everybody says she's a nice kid. Pretty bright, too."

Heimrich said he had noticed that. There was no suggestion that she drank more than was good for her? There was not.

Arnold Thayer was one of the country's outstanding breeders of Aberdeen Angus. He owned a big farm in Missouri, not far from Jefferson City; some of the best Blacks pastured there, and went from there to win prizes on the circuit. He had shown the reserve grand champion at the International show where Deep Meadow Prince had earned his grand championship. He had, at the same show, won the grand championship in the female class with a heifer named, among other things, Bessie. "By and large, from what we hear, he's about the biggest in the business," the county detective said.

Thayer was one of those who had pioneered with Angus; one of those who had done most to popularize the breed, so that on the ranges throughout the country more and more cattle were black, and hornless. He was one of the best known judges in the middle west; he was prominent in the breeders' association.

"No suggestion his judgments have ever been influenced?" Heimrich asked. He got an emphatic shake of the head. "Or that he was ever suspected of sharp practices?"

"None," the county detective said.

"A paragon," Heimrich said.

"He's very well thought of, apparently," the county detective said. "Makes a lot of money out of cattle, too. Good breeder; shrewd business man, from what we hear."

"But," Heimrich said, "Mrs. Landcraft's bull got the grand championship. He'd be an addition even to a farm like you say Thayer's is."

"Apparently," the detective said. "That's about what we've got, captain."

He was told he had got a lot. Heimrich stood up.

"There's one other little thing," the county detective said. "This place Smith died in. The one you found locked and broke open."

"Oh yes," Heimrich said. "That."

"Smith's prints on the padlock," the county detective said. "One of yours overlaying. No others." He regarded Heimrich, looking up from his desk. "We talked to Mrs. Smith. Very upset she is. Not very coherent. She does say they almost never locked up the place. No particular reason to."

"Didn't they?" Heimrich said. "I wondered about that."

"So the man who took Smith there probably wouldn't have found it locked," the detective said. "But, he must have locked it after he put Smith in there. He didn't wipe it off, because Smith's prints are there. But, he had to handle the lock to fasten it. You did when you broke it open, apparently. Things like that puzzle a jury, captain."

"Now Henry," Heimrich said. "He must have worn gloves, naturally."

"Yes," the detective said. "He must have, I guess. But—locking it at all was a damn fool thing to do, wasn't it? Leaving it locked for you to find, since that proved it wasn't suicide. You'd figure he was excited, didn't rightly know what he was doing. But here he is, putting on gloves so as not to leave prints. You can see how a jury might be puzzled, can't you?"

"Yes," Heimrich said. "I can see that, Henry. But—Smith was murdered. Got drunk and murdered. I haven't told anybody he was drunk, by the way."

"Oh," Henry said, "sure."

"And," Heimrich said, "we'll try to make it as simple as we can for the jury. When we get a jury, naturally. Try not to puzzle them."

"If you ask me," the county detective said, "it's puzzling already. Damn puzzling."

"Yes," Heimrich said. "Well. We'll be seeing you, Henry."

He went out of the office, with Ray Crowley after him. In the car, Heimrich said, after looking at his watch, that he thought it might be a good time to have a drink. He said that he gathered there was an inn around somewhere, and to this Ray Crowley agreed, and drove him there. It was an inn which provided accommodations for overnight guests; which had a cocktail lounge; which had leaded panes on windows facing the road. They found the lounge, which was almost empty; they found, in a corner, a table for four. Heimrich ordered bourbon on ice, and looked at the young trooper. "Coke, I guess," Ray said. "I don't drink much, captain." He was told that that was very wise of him.

Heimrich seemed to be in no hurry with his first drink and he was not talkative. He sat, indeed, with his eyes closed. After several minutes, Crowley said that it was a little unfortunate about the fingerprints, and after a long pause, Heimrich agreed it was. "By the way," he said, "we won't mention the point, naturally. Might puzzle people, as Henry says. Or that Smith doesn't seem to have been knocked out." Heimrich thereupon relapsed into what, Ray Crowley thought, a little resembled a coma.

It was, nevertheless, Captain Heimrich who first became conscious that Arnold Thayer had come into the room—was walking across it to the small bar, with its two stools.

(It was only after Heimrich had begun to push the table back a little, part way stand, that Crowley recognized Thayer in the dimly lit room. It was several seconds later that he realized two things—that Thayer had said he was staying at the inn in Carmel; that it was Thayer for whom Heimrich had been waiting.) Thayer paused in his progress toward the bar and looked at Heimrich and Crowley, squinting a little.

"Yes," Heimrich said. "We do get around, Mr. Thayer. Join us, won't you?"

Thayer hesitated.

"As good a place as any," Heimrich said. "May as well be comfortable while we talk."

Thayer did not appear to think that "comfortable" was the word best chosen. He nevertheless came to the table and pulled out a chair. He looked at Heimrich's glass, and Heimrich said, "Bourbon. Not bad."

"Bourbon," Thayer said, to the waiter. "Bourbon and ginger ale."

Heimrich avoided shuddering. Mr. Thayer got what he had asked for.

[illegible]

Where do [illegible]

There [illegible]

that he [illegible]

[illegible]

I don't [illegible]

[illegible]

XII

ARNOLD THAYER HAD heard Smith had been killed. (He drowned good bourbon in ginger ale.) He would have thought it suicide, but no doubt the police had reason for thinking otherwise. (He lighted a corncob pipe, which was unexpected, since he was not dressed for it.) *He* would have thought that Margaret Landcraft had caught the man stealing and threatened to fire him, that the man had become enraged and killed her, that he had killed himself when he realized what he had done and that his effort to make death appear accidental was going to fail.

"You can take it that Smith was murdered," Heimrich said.

"Whatever you say," Thayer's tone was equable. "Well? Where do I come in?"

There was, Heimrich assured him, nothing to indicate that he came in anywhere. There were, however, one or two points. For example—how was his deal to buy Deep Meadow Prince coming along?

"I don't see what that's got to do with it," Thayer said. "Or what business it is of yours." His tone, however, remained undisturbed.

"Now Mr. Thayer," Heimrich said. "It's often hard to tell what my business is, precisely. But I've got to try to get the picture. Need all the help I can get."

"Guess you do," Thayer said. "Well, depends on the boys. I reckon they'll sell, in the end. For my price."

"A low price," Heimrich said.

"Look," Thayer said. "Get this straight, captain. You don't price doddies like you do suits of clothes. The bull's worth what they can get for him. If they think they can do better, that's all right with me."

He was asked to put it this way: If the bull were his, would he sell for thirty thousand?

"Probably not," Thayer said. "All right—sure not. But, I'm a breeder. Harvey Landcraft isn't and doesn't want to be. Wade isn't much of one, and doesn't want to be. They want to get out. Also, the bull's lost value. Nobody wants a mean bull."

"I think the bull was—" Heimrich hesitated for a word. "Well, in a way the bull was framed."

"Maybe," Thayer said. "What people are going to remember—next year, year after next—'that's a mean bull.' If he's prepotent, his get will be mean. If he isn't, what's the good of him? But, it's up to the Landcrafts. I think they want the cash. Harvey needs it, from what I hear. Wade wants to get out of breeding so bad he can taste it."

"He's told you that?"

"His mother did. Or as good as told me."

"You knew Mrs. Landcraft pretty well?"

"Well enough," Thayer said. "Like I know a lot of breeders."

"You were planning to stay at the house," Heimrich said.

"Sure," Thayer said. "Maggie asked me to. Why not?"

"Why?"

"You mean, why did she? Well—" Thayer paused. "O.K.," he said. "If you don't know already, you can find out. I'm pretty well known in the business. Well as anyone. If the sale had gone off, they're a lot would have watched to see what I bought, and what I paid. Say I put up good money for a heifer or two, one of the young bulls maybe. That would get things started the way Maggie wanted them. So—get me feeling friendly. See what I'm getting at?"

"Yes," Heimrich said. "Another drink, Mr. Thayer?"

Thayer hesitated; decided he would have another drink. Heimrich joined him.

"Mrs. Landcraft," Heimrich said, "you'd call her a breeder? In the sense you used the word. The sense Wade Landcraft isn't?"

"Sure," Thayer said. "Also, she had Ballard with her. He's one of the best in the business. I'd take him on any time. Will, probably, if they decide to sell out. He's got the feel of cattle. Put Maggie on to Prince when he was a junior yearling and going cheap. It was Alec brought him along."

Heimrich closed his eyes and leaned back. He said, absently, that he had heard a rumor Mrs. Landcraft was planning to let Ballard go.

"Whoever told you that was crazy," Thayer said. "Unless Maggie'd gone crazy. He could get a better job half a dozen places I know of. Including my place. I said that."

"Why didn't he?"

"Hell," Thayer said. "I don't know. 'Less it was the big bull kept him. Thinks a lot of that bull."

Heimrich sipped. He opened his eyes. He asked whether Mr. Thayer had made an offer for the bull while Mrs. Landcraft was alive.

"Nope," Thayer said. "What would have been the use? Maggie wasn't a fool. If she'd ever thought of selling, she'd have wanted Fort Knox. It's only because things are this way—" He had held his glass as he started the sentence; now he set it down, abruptly, on the table. He looked hard at Heimrich.

"Yes," Heimrich said. "Mrs. Landcraft's death changed things, naturally."

"Look," Thayer said, and now his manner changed a little, his tone was no longer casual. "Look, mister. You wouldn't be trying to say—anything. Would you?"

"Now Mr. Thayer," Heimrich said. "Such as what?"

"I wouldn't know," Thayer said. "Tell you how it is: I wouldn't want to know. See what I mean?"

Heimrich said he saw what Mr. Thayer meant. He said, "Take it easy, Mr. Thayer," but Thayer finished his drink in a gulp. He said, "Well?" challengingly.

"Nothing," Heimrich said. "Thanks, Mr. Thayer. You've been helpful."

"Think so?" Thayer said. "Think so if you want to." He stood up.

"Going over to the Landcrafts' now," he said. "Get their answer on the bull. That all right with you?"

He exaggerated the question.

"Now Mr. Thayer," Heimrich said. "Why not?"

"Whatever the answer is, I'm going home tomorrow," Thayer said. "You get that, mister?"

"Yes," Heimrich said. "I heard you, Mr. Thayer."

Thayer turned away, and walked away. Crowley and Heimrich watched him.

"Stirred him up at the end," Crowley said.

"Yes," Heimrich said. "It did seem that way, Ray. Well, stirring them up's useful, sometimes."

Heimrich looked at his watch. It showed six-thirty, and that was a later hour than Heimrich had expected, although an early hour for dinner.

"What do you think, Ray?" Heimrich asked. "Likely to be another fog tonight?"

Ray Crowley got up and walkd to a window and looked out into the clear evening. He came back and said he shouldn't think so.

Then, Heimrich said, they might as well have something to eat, and he enquired of the bartender. They could eat in the bar. They ordered, and ordered steaks.

The steaks were a long time in coming; time at the inn was not, apparently, of the essence. Heimrich, waiting, had another drink. It was clear enough; should have been clear from the first. It was going to be difficult to prove, however, unless things went just right. It was unfortunate he had left a fingerprint on the padlock—or that the murderer of William Smith had not. Probably, of course, the other had never touched the lock.

The steaks came, finally. They were not, Heimrich decided, cut from Angus steers.

It is difficult to remember how the days shorten by mid-September, how even with daylight saving time they shorten. The warmth, which may be almost that of midsummer—which that day had been—misleads.

It was dark when they left the inn. It was also foggy. The spaced street lights of Carmel's main street were softly wrapped in fog, glowing dimly.

"You're not a very good weather prophet, Ray," Heimrich said, and his tone was mild. But his blue eyes were very wide open, and he moved toward the car at much more than his accustomed pace. "The wind changed," Ray said, going around the car.

"Yes," Heimrich said. "We want to get back as fast as we can, Ray."

The sedan had fog lights—amber lights, set low, their beams hugging the ground. They helped, but in fog nothing helps enough. It was not too difficult while they were still in the village, where street lights, however watery, paled the gray darkness. It was very difficult on the winding road which led them out of Carmel. Wipers swished at the dampness which formed on the windshield; formed and was whisked away, but formed again before the hurrying blades could retraverse their arcs.

"See why Miss Merritt couldn't identify the men," Ray Crowley said, going at twenty-five—which was fast for the night—hugging the center of the black-surfaced road. "Lucky to see them at all."

"Or," Heimrich said, "unlucky, Ray. How long do you figure to get back?"

Half an hour might do it, Ray Crowley thought.

"Three quarters, more likely," Heimrich said. He rolled down the window on his side of the car, leaned out of it. It was surprising—it was always surprising—what a difference the absence of windshield glass made; it was surprising how much one could see through fog, providing always one did not look ahead into the light which danced back from the air's vapor. "It's longer than I like, Ray. But—probably it will be—"

He stopped abruptly. They were going around a curve, down an incline. Ahead of them, in the middle of the road, the lights of another car peered at them—peered myopically, grew brighter. The horn of the police car blared, in warning, in anger; Ray wrenched the wheel around, the car swerved to the right. Ray added his voice to the horn's harsh hooting, condemning with fury all drivers from cities, hogging country roads on foggy nights.

The approaching car veered right, finally, but too late. The police car went to the shoulder, and the shoulder was soft. The car yawed in unpacked earth, and Ray fought it. The other car passed, clearing by inches. Ray braked and they skidded. Then, joltingly, they stopped. A front tire blew, sharply.

"Hit a culvert," Ray said, and added to what he had said about the other driver.

They got out with flashlights and looked at things, and things frowned back. They had hit the edge of a culvert, and the tire was done. The wheel was dished. There was, also, no place to put a jack.

It was slow work, backing first to the road again, while Heimrich waved a flashlight in warning; edging then on the road's surface, lurching as the car edged, around the culvert and off the road again onto the yielding shoulder. The jack slewed twice under the front bumper; the damaged wheel was jammed in place, and it took them both to wrench it off—and if the car slipped from the jack while they wrenched, it was going to be too bad all around. It just didn't, which was a small favor to give thanks for.

It had been a quarter of eight when they left the inn. It was after nine when they had the spare tire on and could start again. They had covered two miles of a dozen, and the fog had thickened. They crept through it.

Heimrich's fingers played a soundless tune on the top of the instrument panel, as he leaned forward, peering into the fog. Things could hardly have gone more completely wrong. He looked at the microphone through which he could summon help. But—they were as close as anyone, and could move as fast. Close enough and moving fast enough? There was no way of telling that. Heimrich was not a man who often rebelled against impersonal obstacles, but now, inwardly, he cursed the fog.

He had taken a chance, but one had to take chances. And the plan had been good. By now—long before now—Thayer would have reached the Landcraft house; inevitably he would have mentioned their meeting at the inn; mentioned that he had left policemen there, obviously intending to have dinner there. To someone who would hear him, the relaxed position of policemen would be highly encouraging. All according to plan—but not the fog. Not the venomous, the inscrutable, fog.

"We want to make as good time as we can, Ray," Heimrich said, mildly. "We don't want to be late."

"I don't—" Ray Crowley began, his attention all on the road, which seemed to waver in front of them.

"At the Merritts', Ray," Heimrich said. "That wouldn't be so good, naturally."

XIII

SHE SAT WITH a book in her bedroom, dressed in shirt and shorts, and held the book in front of her eyes, and did not see the pages. She saw two men, one taller than the other, standing by the roadside in the fog, behind a small car. She saw a broad-shouldered man, heavily built, walking as if he would walk through anything. She heard the disbelief in Heimrich's voice when, on the terrace, he had asked, not for the first time, whether she was sure she had recognized neither of the men by the road.

And again she tried, as she had tried so many times in recent hours, to see the men as she had seen them then. It was evident, now, that one of the men had been Smith—must have been Smith. The police, unless they had been sure, would not have drained the quarry pool. That they had not found Smith's body there, but had found it elsewhere, did not matter. They had been certain that Smith and the man with him had stopped there, and that the pool might have been the place chosen for Smith's death. The plan had changed, but only in method. Smith had died. The change in method—that must have been decided on because she had seen the two together.

So—one of the men had been Smith. She forced her mind back to the scene; stared at the book as if she were looking again into the fog of the night before and could drive her vision through it. The small man was Smith—the small man was Smith. If knowing that now, she could *see* the man as Smith, then she might see the other man. It might all come back. Then she could go to Heimrich and tell him who it was—tell him it wasn't Wade. That was what mattered—who the man was not, not who he was. He could be—all right, he could be anybody, but not Wade. A stranger would be best—would be infinitely best. But if not a stranger, than *anybody,* excepting only Wade. She *had* to remember. It *had* to come back. She would make it come back.

Knowledge was somewhere there, under the surface. She had passed close to the men; subconsciously, she must have recognized them, or known that she did not recognize them. The surprise of coming so close on to them, the shock of concentration in avoiding them, had driven the picture of them under the surface. Well then, she would bring it up. The car had been so—she could see the car. The men—

Evelyn was in the "birthday room"; the room which had been given her when she became eighteen; the room she had come home from school to find waiting. It was on the ground floor of the house, and when she was growing up it had been her father's workroom. He had had a lathe in it, and she could remember the shrieks which used to come from the room, as a power saw bit through wood. (She could remember, also, the yells of pain and outrage which had come from it, on one fall evening, when the rotating, impartial saw had nipped off the end of her father's right forefinger. She could remember, Evelyn thought, everything but the thing she had to remember.)

The room had been changed beyond recognition when she came home from school the summer of her eighteenth birthday. It had been made much longer; one side had become a wall of windows, which slid in tracks; could, in very hot weather, be lifted out entirely. At the end of the room, where there had been a single narrow door, there were french doors, opening onto a small terrace of the room's own—a terrace shielded on one side by a windowless wall of the house, on the other by an evergreen hedge. The french doors could be locked from outside, as well as from within, and the symbol of the room had been the two keys to the lock—both of the keys, not merely one. When you can lock your own door, a door opens wide—if you are eighteen.

"Had enough of you tramping up the stairs when you come back from dates," her father had told her sternly. "Never could see how such a small girl could make such a racket. Wake us up at all hours."

But the stairs were heavily carpeted, and Evelyn moved lightly.

—one of the men had been Smith. The other had been much taller. Had he been—yes, he had been hatless. He had been wearing— But it broke down there. She went back. He had been standing with an arm around the shoulders of the shorter man; he had looked at the lights momentarily, his face a white blur, and then away again. The blur had been—

She laid the book down and pressed against her temples

with the heels of her thumbs. The blur had been a face—a face—a *face*. She would make the face come out of the fog, drag it up out of the fog. She would—

There was a small, sharp sound from the end of the room, where the french doors opened on the terrace. The sound was repeated. It was as if tips of branches, moving gently in the breeze, were tapping at the glass.

The sound was repeated several times, but not more loudly the last times than the first, before it broke into the concentration of the girl who was driving memory into fog. She was aware of it first as an annoyance, an intrusion. She tried to close her ears to it. But when it was once more repeated, the sound acquired meaning. Someone was tapping at the glass of one of the doors; tapping softly, with finger tips, the nails of the fingers clicking on the glass.

She looked up, and toward the end of the room. There was a shadow there, but as she looked up, sitting under the reading lamp, the shadow receded. She shook her head slightly, and then got up and walked to the doors. She switched on a lamp near the doors, and light went out through the doors, and was hazy on the terrace. There was fog again.

Just where the light died against the fog, a man was standing and, when he saw that she had seen him, the man beckoned. He was tall and indistinct in the fog and, after he had beckoned, he patted his lips with the fingers of one hand, signaling silence.

Then Evelyn, although still the man was a blur, decided it was Wade. The disreputable hat of his, worn for the most part in the barns, worn tonight obviously because of the dampness in the air, was unmistakable.

He often came around the house to her special door, but he had before come only by daylight—had come on sunny mornings and sunny afternoons, his car parked in the drive beyond the terrace; had come to drive her into the city for lunch and a matinee; to drive her slowly, lazily, on back roads which led nowhere and did not need to, since the two in the car carried their destination with them.

But it was different now. Now he came at night, and not openly. The tapping on the glass had been a veiled tapping, stealthy. It had been for her ears only, for her secret ears. The gestures, first to tell her to join him, then to come silently, had been abrupt and urgent. He was disturbed. (Wade's movements commonly were smooth, unhurried; his brother was the quick one, the urgent one.)

When he realized he had been seen, his gestures recognized, the man withdrew further into the fog, avoiding light. But she could still see him, dimly, as a kind of darkness outlined on darkness. She turned to a chest by the doors and started to open it, reaching for a flashlight. But, as she did so, the man outside threw a circle of brightness on the flags of the terrace. Wade was telling her that he had a flash, that she would not need one.

She opened the door, then, and opened it quietly. The light, crepe-soled shoes on her bare feet made no sound on the flagstones. The air was wet and cool and she shivered, but only partly from the dampness, and colder air. She closed the door behind her, as quietly as she could, and she whispered, "*Wade?*"

There was no answer. But again, very briefly, the circle of light from the flash, pointed directly downward, was on the flagstones. This time, it moved away from her, and so it beckoned.

The implication was obvious. They were too close to the house—to her father and mother, and the servants, in the house. They must talk secretly, and not there. The light went out, and she heard his footsteps on the gravel of the drive. She heard them only for a moment, and then, as she followed, she realized that he had stepped from the gravel and its telltale sound, to the lawn which bordered the drive. To show her that, the light appeared again, on gravel now. It moved away from her.

She had to cross the drive to reach the silent grass, and did so as carefully as she could, as soundlessly. On the grass, she followed after. There was tightness in her throat; there seemed to be a band around her chest, constricting, making her breathing shallow. Because all this could mean— She tried not to think what it could mean, but the knowledge was heavy in her mind.

Something had happened—something again had happened. It involved Wade, made it necessary that he move secretly. It had brought him to her because he needed her. Or because—because— If Wade had to go away, had to run in the night, he could come to her first. He would come to say goodbye. Whatever had happened, he would do that. Whatever he had done.

She could not see him now, even as darkness moving on in darkness, nor hear the sound of his feet on the grass. But she was certain he still was moving ahead of her, and that he must now, as they walked beside the drive, toward the road, be moving more quickly. So she moved more quickly, too. The wetness of the grass soaked through the thin fabric of her shoes; with the wetness in the air, her thin shirt clung to her. It was clammy and, as she moved, she half-consciously plucked at the shirt, holding it out from her body. But when she released the material, it fell back and clung to her, coldly.

As she neared the road, she peered through the fog, expecting to see Wade's car parked near the driveway entrance. That must be what he had in mind; that they should get into the car and drive slowly and then, where they could not be overheard, he would—would tell her.

But she could not see the car, nor, in the drive entrance, between the low pillars of the wall which ran along the road, could she see Wade, although that, surely, was where he would stop and wait for her. She went on and now, far enough from the house, she spoke again, softly. "Wade?" she said. "Where—"

She was seized from behind—seized harshly, roughly, a heavy hand on either of her shoulders. There was violence in the hands, and she tried to scream, and one of the hands clasped bruisingly over her mouth. She was forced back against the man behind her. The hand which had been brutally hard on her mouth moved toward her throat.

She struggled, then—struggled wildly. She clutched at the threatening hand, and twisted in a kind of frenzy and knew, while she threw her head back, hoping to beat with it against the man's face, that she struggled hopelessly. Held as she was, she could not—

And then, unbelievably, as she tore at the hand on her throat, she loosened its grip. The hand seemed, suddenly, to go lax, and then, with all her strength, she twisted her body and the hand which held her shoulder slipped on the wet cloth of her shirt and for an instant she was free. She leaped away, and the hands clutched again, and fastened on the cloth. But the cloth of the shirt tore in the grasping hands, and Evelyn ran.

She ran without hope, could almost feel the hands closing on her, but she ran with desperation. She ran straight on, down the drive, between the pillars, across the hard surface of the road. She stumbled on the uneven surface, caught herself staggeringly, and went on. She clawed her way up the bank beyond, and over the low wall at its top; forced her way through bushes which tore at her, whipped her legs.

As she ran across the road, the beam of a flashlight from behind sought her out. But it was dim in the fog; she was only half conscious of it—half conscious that its light had helped her find her way up the bank and to the wall. The light went out as she went over the wall.

Wade's trying to kill me, she thought as she ran down the slope beyond the wall, ran through high-growing goldenrod. *Wade's trying to kill me.* It was Wade with Smith and he thinks I'll remember and—

* * *

They groped very slowly over a rise in Old Road and the amber lights picked up again the black wetness of the road. Roads and fog had seemed without end. "Pretty close, now," Ray Crowley said. "I—" He stopped.

Ahead—perhaps a hundred feet ahead—there had been sudden movement in the fog. It was movement from left to right across the road—a flicker of movement, as if denser but brighter fog had moved through fog. "See that?" Crowley asked, and his voice was low.

"Something running across the road," Heimrich said. "Yes. I saw it."

"A deer?" Ray said. "Tail up? Running? There're a lot around."

"I don't know," Heimrich said. "I hope so. But—let's stop here, Ray."

Crowley pulled the car to the right, onto the narrow shoulder. "About the same place, isn't it?" he said, and Crowley said it was. "Better cut the lights," Heimrich said. "I don't think it was a deer, Ray. The girl, I think. We'd better find out, hadn't we?"

Ray Crowley took a deep breath, and Heimrich spoke quickly. "No," he said. "Don't call her. She wasn't running for fun, you know. She was running from something, naturally. Can we get through here, Ray?"

They could. They could get up a bank, over a low stone fence. Ray used his flashlight briefly, and Heimrich said, "No. Not unless we're pretty sure." They went into the gray darkness, their eyes adjusting slowly. "Moon's up," Ray said. It helped a little; the fog had now a kind of translucence. But it seemed, despite that, thicker than before.

They were in the field of goldenrod again. Moving through it, they were almost at once coldly wet. They separated in the field, so that they were moving, more or less in parallel, but a hundred feet or so apart. Ray had gone to his left; he was about, he thought, where the runner must have entered the field.

Both the men moved very slowly, stopping often to listen. After a time, they managed so that they stopped together, and thus made sure that any sound of movement heard was not their own. But it was a long time, as they moved through the field, toward the quarry cliff, before they heard anything.

* * *

She crouched low in the goldenrod and she was shaking—with cold, with fear and with something worse than fear. She listened for the movements of the man who was trying to kill her. She had only her ears. That had been seen to. One flashlight would do for both, a gesture had said. And she had trusted.

The sound was very slight, when she finally heard it. It was the faintest swishing of the tall-growing weeds against clothing; a damp, secret sound. It was coming toward her. The sound stopped, and she knew that the man had stopped, to listen—as she listened. The sound began again and, as it did, she moved. She had come straight in from the road; now she moved off toward her right. The ground began to rise, here; she was going up the slope of the hill into which the quarry had been driven. As she moved now, the sheer cliff of the quarry's high side would be to her left—somewhere to her left.

She stopped again and listened. At first she heard nothing. The man—*and the man was Wade*—had stopped again, was listening again. She crouched low. What remained of her white shirt would, even in the fog, betray her to anyone close enough. And—when he was close enough, he would use the light. Not yet. Now it would reveal more to her than to him. But—when he was close enough. When he was ready.

There was sound again, but now it confused her. It seemed to come from two places, very faintly through the damp night. Her ears played tricks, she thought; the fog played tricks, or the contour of the land. Wade was, as now she crouched facing back toward the road, on her left, as well as on her right. He was everywhere in the night.

It's in my mind, she thought. It's all broken up in my mind. The sound stopped—the sound and the echo of the sound. She waited. The sound to her left resumed.

She turned and went again, gropingly, through the goldenrod. It had been easy enough before; the light stalks parted readily. But now the foliage dragged at her; it seemed to require all her strength to move away from death. She was, she thought, moving with each step more slowly. She stopped again to listen, and heard the sound again—and the echo of the sound. The sound was closer.

And ahead, now, was the cliff's edge. He was driving her toward the cliff. It was ahead—but was it ahead? She stopped again. In the fog nothing differed from any other thing. There was nothing familiar. Was the cliff ahead? Or to her right—or her left? I'm lost, she thought. I don't know which way to turn. I've got out of bed in a dark room and lost the way and this wall is wrong and the door is gone and—

That's panic, she thought. Don't panic.

She went on.

* * *

The girl's going toward the cliff, Heimrich thought. If it is the girl, and it's the girl all right.

He couldn't, he realized, chance it much longer. He

would have to call to her. Probably thinks it's the man who's after her, Heimrich thought. If she hears us at all, and probably she does, since we can hear her. If it is her.

That was the point. It might be the man they wanted; the man who was supposed to be around, doing just what he evidently was doing. If they called to the girl, identified themselves, she would be all right. And so would the man they were after—the man who had been so lucky (so *damned* lucky) with the weather.

Only, Heimrich thought, moving through the high weeds, he won't be all right. For now—yes. We won't pick him up while he's at it; wind it up quick and neat and according to plan. He—

Heimrich heard two sounds then, in quick succession. One was a car starting up on the road behind him. It had been, from the sound, parked beyond the Merritt driveway. That would have been the place. The man had doubled back and— Heimrich swore, under his breath. The man hadn't crossed the road at all. He'd started the girl running, seen the police car stop, waited until they had had time to get deep into the field, and then got in the car and driven away. Very neat.

Then Heimrich heard the second sound. It was the high scream of a woman in terror.

* * *

For the final seconds—but they did not seem like seconds; they had no measurement in time—she had walked through the goldenrod dazedly. All thought had stopped; reality had failed. Flight and fear were at once meaningless. She went on to no purpose; the fog was in her mind.

Then the ground moved under her foot, and seemed to

fall away ahead of her, carrying her with it. For an instant even this seemed a dream, but then the dream broke. She screamed, and clutched wildly about her, as earth broke away from the top of the cliff; fell away toward the quarry pool, toward the rocks at the surface of black water.

One flung-out hand found something—a branch, a root—and her body's weight wrenched at her shoulder. She was hanging over the edge of the cliff, and the thing she clutched seemed to be fighting to free itself from her grasp. She screamed again, and heard a man shout somewhere, and the sound of running.

He was coming to finish it. She might as well let go—let it all go. But, instead, she found the support—it was a tree root, exposed by the falling away of the cliff's lip—with her other hand, and clung desperately with both. When he came, he would break her hold. She would fall into the darkness.

But he would have to break the hold. If he was to kill her, let him use his hands—his hands on hers. Let him feel death—don't let him off—don't—

A light was around her, on her hands. A man was lying on the ground above her, reaching down. *You have to do it, Wade! I won't do it for you!*

Hands closed on her wrists. "*Hold on,*" a man said. "*Got you, Evvie!*"

But still, the hands on her wrists now supporting most of her weight, she dangled there, above the water and the rocks. Then she felt herself lifted up, dragged up and forward and finally across the ground. The ground hurt, bruisingly. She tried to roll to her back, and instead was lifted up, carried for a step or two, put down on her feet.

There were two men, and she looked up at the man who had held her.

"Why," she said. "*Ray! It isn't–* Was it you all the–"

"No," Heimrich said. "It wasn't Ray all the time, Miss Merritt."

She put her hands over her face, then, and began to cry—to cry harshly.

"Put a coat around her, Ray," Heimrich said. "You recognized the man, Miss Merritt?"

She took her hands down, then. She started to shake her head.

"Now Miss Merritt," Heimrich said. "You recognized the man this time, didn't you?"

She looked up at him, light from the flash on her face. She started to speak and failed. Her face was set. Heimrich waited.

She did not speak the name that pounded in her mind. But—finally, slowly—she nodded her head.

"Yes," Heimrich said. "I thought you'd recognize him, this time."

XIV

THEY HAD TAKEN her back, across the road, to the Merritt house. It was at her insistence that they had moved quietly, not arousing her parents. She said, dully, that nobody could help her do it; Heimrich had guessed that she was avoiding, defensively, any emotional pressure which would break a temporary anesthesia of the mind. They waited, in the house, for her to dress.

"Practically unchanged," Heimrich said, as if to himself, and Ray Crowley looked at him in the dim light and waited. Heimrich's eyes were closed. "The key word is 'practically.'" Crowley continued to wait; he was learning. "The catalytic agent, Ray," Heimrich said. "You often find it. You know what it is?"

"Not precisely," Crowley said.

"No," Heimrich said. "Probably I don't either. Except for the definition. A substance used by chemists—any one of a good many substances, I suppose. You put it with other substances and it 'accelerates a reaction,' the definition says. But it is not involved in the reaction. It can be recovered afterward 'practically unchanged.' This time it's the girl, Ray. In it, but not actually of it. Accelerating the reaction. But, whether she can be 'recovered practically unchanged'—I don't know, Ray."

"You planned it that way?"

"Now Ray. It wasn't my plan, naturally. All I did was—shape it a little."

He was told that he had taken a chance. He agreed that, as things turned out, he apparently had. But the formation of earth and rock at the edge of a cliff, a lack of tenacity in nature—that could not have been anticipated.

"I didn't mean that, sir," Crowley said, and was told that Heimrich knew he didn't. It had, however, been the greatest peril.

"Not Landcraft?"

Heimrich opened his eyes and looked at Ray Crowley. After a moment he smiled faintly and shook his head.

"Not the way you mean," he said. "I don't think you quite get it, Ray. I didn't myself—or not all of it. It's based on an old saying—or part of it. 'The wicked flee when no man pursueth.' But—so may the innocent. Depends on circumstances. If—"

He was interrupted. Evelyn Merritt came into the room and stood just inside and waited. She had changed to a dark slack suit, a thin sweater under the jacket. Her face was very pale. There was little expression in her eyes. "I'm ready," she said.

The two men stood up.

"I'm sorry, Miss Merritt," Heimrich said. "We do need you."

"You told me," she said. "Shall we get it over, captain?"

The youth had gone out of her voice. Only the texture of youth remained, and seemed false. There was, Heimrich thought, another old saying having to do with the making of omelets—a very harsh saying, however homely its form. Heimrich did not much care for the saying, or for its implications. But he cared less for murder.

There was no hurry, now. Ray Crowley drove the car slowly in the luminous fog. As gently as he could, Heimrich got details of the story from Evelyn Merritt—of the brief, violent story, which had begun with a tapping on glass like the tapping of branches swaying in a gentle breeze.

"You knew who it was?" Heimrich said. "That was the reason you went out, naturally."

She used the name, then, for the first time.

"It was Wade," she said.

"You saw his face? The fog blurs things."

"He came the way he always did," the girl said. "I knew who it was."

"At once?"

"What's the use?" the girl said. "I don't remember—yes—it was that hat he wears. At first. Of course, afterward, it was—oh, everything. How does one know a person?"

"He got behind you and grabbed you and you—broke loose?"

"Yes. His hands slipped, somehow."

"And you ran."

"Oh yes," she said. "I ran. Do—do I have to see him, captain?"

"Yes," Heimrich said. "All of them, Miss Merritt. Because—we can't have murder, naturally. I know it will be difficult. You'll do it as I said?"

(*You love a man and he tries to kill you. You point a finger; say, "That's the man." And the word is "difficult"!*)

She nodded her head, but did not say anything. Crowley turned the car up the Landcraft driveway. The house was larger in the fog. It seemed to waver in the fog. Crowley stopped the car behind another in the turnaround and Heimrich walked to the other car and felt the radiator cowling. It was just perceptibly warm. Of course, it had not been run far. It had, also, had time to cool. They went to the door, the girl between them, and Harvey Landcraft came to the door after a few seconds. He said, "Well, hello. Hello, Evvie." He looked at her again. "You all right?" he asked.

"She's all right, Mr. Landcraft," Heimrich said. "Had an unpleasant experience, but she's all right now. Your brother around?"

"Sure," Harvey said. He gestured them in. "You want to talk to him?"

"All of you," Heimrich said.

He was told that Bonita, if he meant her also, had gone to bed. Heimrich was sorry. He wanted all of them. "Including," he said, "Mr. Ballard. Mr. Thayer, if he's still here."

Harvey Landcraft hesitated. Heimrich merely looked at him. "O.K.," Harvey said. "You're the boss, apparently. Thayer's in the library."

"Yes," Heimrich said.

They found Thayer in the library. Thayer said, "Again, eh?" and, "Evening, Miss Merritt." Harvey left; after a time returned.

"Bonny'll be along," he said. "I called Ballard. Wade's around somewhere. Probably—"

There was a sound from the hall. "Wade?" Harvey

called, and Wade Landcraft answered. He came into the room. He was wearing the battered felt hat, and took it off and held it for a moment, and put it down on a chair. He did not, at once, seem to see Evelyn Merritt; looked at Heimrich. He said, "Well. You again."

Then he saw Evelyn, and moved into the room and held out both hands toward her and said, "Evvie!" She did not move from the chair. "You all right?" he asked, the words quick.

"Why shouldn't she be, Mr. Landcraft?" Heimrich said. "I want you to hear—all of you to hear—about something that happened to her. But—she's all right."

Wade moved toward the girl.

"Wait," Heimrich said. "Sit down, won't you? When the—"

Bonita came into the room, then. She wore a house coat; only a house coat, Heimrich decided. She was a very pretty young woman. She looked a little sleepy.

"The damned police, the damned police, the damned police are here," she sang to a fraction of a tune which was older than she. She looked around. "Oh," she said. "Trouble." She looked at Evelyn. She said, "Darling, you look terrible," and went to the other girl and sat on the arm of her chair. "Tell mamma."

Evelyn smiled with her lips. She shook her head and looked at Heimrich. Only his eyes moved. They said, "Not yet."

Ballard was the last. He wore corduroy trousers and a light windbreak, zipped over what appeared to be the top of yellow pajamas. He smoothed his hair down as he stood in the doorway. He said, to Harvey, "You wanted me?"

"Miss Merritt has something to tell us," Heimrich said. "Something I want you all to hear. All right, Miss Merritt."

The voice, to her own ears, was another's voice—expressionless, plodding. She spoke slowly; it was as if each word had to be individually remembered. "I was sitting reading a book and someone—" She did not look around; looked only at Heimrich, who sat a little detached from the others, with the light on his face. But she did not really see Heimrich. "I went out and—"

She paused, because someone had spoken. She heard Heimrich say, "Later. Go on, Miss Merritt."

Each word was dry in her mouth. "—from behind. I—" The scene was not, in her own mind, re-created. There were words to say. "—ran across and—" But she did not feel herself running; did not re-endure the minutes—which were seconds; which were hours—in the field of goldenrod. "—the ground gave way and I started—" Her shoulders ached still from the strain of her body's weight against her desperate hands; her hands were bruised. Someone else's shoulders; another person's hands. She finished. She stopped. Then she looked down at the hands lying loosely in her lap. She heard someone swear. It was over. But there was no feeling that anything was over.

It was not over.

"You recognized this man, Miss Merritt?"

She looked up again, looked at Captain Heimrich. She nodded her head slowly. He had wanted it this way; wanted this held until the end. One way was as good as another.

"Who was it?"

The word was no more difficult than any other word, no harder to say and no easier, no dryer in the mouth.

"Wade," she said. "It was Wade."

Now it was over. She looked down again at her hands. Dully, she felt that Wade Landcraft was looking at her across the room; dully she knew that he had started to get to his feet, and that Heimrich had stopped him with a gesture. But these things happened far away, dimly.

"You're sure?"

She nodded her head.

She heard her name, spoken sharply, with demand. It was Wade's voice. "Listen to me, Evvie. Listen to me. No. No, Evvie. It wasn't—" She did not look at him. "*Listen to me!*" She listened, did not hear. But she heard the words.

"You deny it, naturally," Heimrich said. "I take it you do, Mr. Landcraft?"

She did not hear an answer; Wade had merely nodded his head.

"She saw you."

"She couldn't have," Wade said. "I was nowhere near. I wouldn't hurt Evvie—not Evvie. Beyond anybody. Don't you see that?"

He seemed to speak to Heimrich. But, although she did not look up, she could feel his eyes on her; feel—but dimly, from behind the fogged glass which separated her from the others—the demand in his gaze, and in his voice.

"No," Heimrich said. "I'm afraid I don't, Mr. Landcraft. I'm afraid it all hangs together very well."

She would not listen any more; there was nothing more to be said that mattered. But still she heard the words.

"It all adds up," Heimrich said, and spoke slowly and was not interrupted. "Your mother—for money, to get away from a life you hated."

(That was not the word, she thought; it did not matter, but the word was wrong. No—it must have been right. She had not thought Wade hated the life at Deep Meadow, but only that he was restless there, unsatisfied. But, he must have hated it. She had been wrong there, too—wrong about hate as about love.)

"—wanted to sell out," Heimrich said. "To get away. Your mother wouldn't sell. Her life was here. And so her death was, naturally."

Still Wade did not speak.

"Then Smith," Heimrich said. "Did he see something, Mr. Landcraft? Threaten to tell what he had seen? Or—was it merely to give us someone, when you realized we were going to get someone? A murderer who committed suicide. It could have been that simple, naturally."

Wade did not speak. Perhaps slowly, hopelessly, he shook his head again. She did not look to see.

"Murder without hate, as Mrs. Landcraft said." Heimrich's voice went on, heavy, uninflected, without emotion. She supposed that it had to be this way; that all which was obvious had to be said in words, spelled out. She heard the words. "A little man of no importance. A man who—"

"Listen, mister," Alec Ballard's voice said. "I don't know about the rest. Got it right, I guess. But—nobody would kill Smitty just for that. Get him drunk and put him in that place—just to get yourself out of something."

There was a pause, then, but it was brief.

"You don't think so, Mr. Ballard?" Heimrich said. "It's hard to tell what people will do. Sometimes I think—" He let the sentence hang, started over. "Perhaps Smith saw something," he said. "Saw too much. It doesn't matter a great deal. He was killed. Got drunk, as you say, Mr. Ballard, and put in the pump house to die. It looked like a tomb. I thought that when I first—"

(The numbness was wearing away a little; words were eroding it. Would he go on forever? Was there never an end? Would he say over and over what was obvious—that Wade had killed, and killed again, and tried once more to kill?)

"You got him drunk," Heimrich said, and it was clear that he still spoke to Wade—spoke inexorably to Wade. But she did not look at Wade, did not look at anyone. "The first plan was to push him over the quarry cliff, of course. But—you were seen, or thought you were. Identified—or thought you were. It didn't make much difference which, as long as you doubted. *Miss Merritt.*"

She heard him, looked up at him.

"Again," he said. "You say you didn't recognize the men by the car last night? You still say that?"

She nodded her head, and looked down again at her hands.

"But you couldn't know," Heimrich said. "There was that doubt. A frightening doubt, naturally. She might be lying, for some reason. Most likely to protect someone. And—whom would she protect? We come to that, don't we? Only one man, of course. But, even that man—how long? We come to that too. It's hard to believe a man will kill his mother. Maybe Miss Merritt couldn't make herself believe it. Kept on hoping, as people do. But after Smith—well, there wasn't any doubt about that. If she'd recognized the man, she'd have told then—or told soon. Whoever he was."

(On and on he went; heavily, spelling it out. Why didn't he get it over with? When it was over with she could go— But it didn't matter where she went.)

"So the attack on Miss Merritt," Heimrich said. "That turned out to be the next step, naturally. To make sure. Things hadn't worked out as they'd been planned. Mrs. Landcraft's death wasn't taken as accident, as it was supposed to have been. When I found the pump house locked from the outside, Smith's death wasn't suicide. So—there had to be another step. What happened tonight. Because—"

"No," Wade said. "I tell you, *no!* I was nowhere near there. Down at the barns, getting the bulls in. They'd been put out, as usual, and I looked down and they were still out—in the fog. So—"

"Now Mr. Landcraft," Heimrich said. "In the barns? Wearing that hat?"

He pointed to the hat on the chair.

"I don't know," Wade said. "What about the hat?"

"Oh," Heimrich said, "Miss Merritt recognized your hat, Mr. Landcraft. It's quite recognizable. One of the ways she knew it was you. The hat was unmistakable, even in the fog."

"I don't—" Wade said, and stopped, and when he spoke again there was a new note in his voice. "No, I wasn't," he said. "Picked it up off the nail in the big barn when I came through on my way—" But the new note faded.

"What's the use?" he said. "You've got it all added up and–"

"No," Harvey Landcraft said, and there was a sharpness in his voice that startled Evelyn, so that she looked at him, and saw he was leaning forward under a light. "It doesn't all add, captain. Because–*why is Evvie still alive?*"

It was only that; it had been foolish to think it was any more than that.

"Why, Mr. Landcraft," Heimrich said. "She told us that. She struggled, got loose. She's an active young woman, obviously. Hard to hold on to anybody who wants to get away bad enough."

"And ran and got away?" Harvey said. "From a man Wade's size? Who had a flashlight? Hell, captain, don't you–"

"I'll tell you," Alec Ballard said, "the captain's right, Mr. Landcraft. Likely you haven't had much experience. But you get anybody who's real scared and tries real hard–Hell, I've had trouble holding on to a scared cat. You wouldn't know, living in the city. Ask anybody's been around animals–Mr. Thayer over there."

There was a long pause. And now, although it was nothing–a thing meaningless in itself, a detail unduly stressed–Evelyn looked across the room at Arnold Thayer, who sat in a shadow and who remained in a shadow, who said:

"Wouldn't know, Alec. No use bringing me into it." He paused. "Or trying to," he said. "Actually, no point I can see in my staying around. So–"

"No," Heimrich said. "We're about done, Mr. Thayer. Stay around."

"Captain," Bonita Landcraft said. *"Listen to Harvey. Don't you see?"*

"Now Mrs. Landcraft," Heimrich said. "See? Go on, Mrs. Landcraft."

She said, "Harv?"

"All right," Harvey Landcraft said. "If Evvie got killed, she couldn't identify Wade, could she? But, if she was grabbed, and let go and chased a little way, she could identify the one who did it, couldn't she? Or—*the kind of hat he was wearing.*"

(She was awake, now. There was a wild hurrying in her mind. The hat—*but of course it was Wade!* He had come as he often came, to the locked door of her room. He had stood outside on the terrace as he often stood, and— *But it had been the hat which had made her certain.* The rest had come afterward. It had been—)

"Expecting it to be Wade because, I imagine, he often went to this door of hers," Harvey said. "Seeing the hat—it's a hell of a hat, Wade. And, from that, everything falling together, or seeming to, so that—"

"Tell you what it is, Mr. Landcraft," Alec Ballard said. "You ought to write stories. Know how you feel but, hell, you try to hold on to somebody who's scared and you'd find out. Even a guy as little as Smitty, you'd—"

He stopped, and there was suddenly a very heavy silence in the room. The silence lay there for seconds, and something sang in Evelyn Merritt's mind.

"Yes, Mr. Ballard," Heimrich said, and spoke slowly. "Even a guy as little as Smitty. Even when he was drunk, probably. When he heard the padlock snap and—"

Alec Ballard was standing up; he stepped toward Heimrich.

"You're crazy," he said. "What the hell you saying, mister? If you think you can pull another frame-up on—"

But once more he stopped, and now, at a signal from Heimrich, Ray Crowley moved beside the big man. And Heimrich stood, too.

"*Another* frame-up, Ballard?" Heimrich said. "There was only one, you know. But—*how* do you know, Ballard? The door wasn't locked, until I locked it. That was a frame. Murder framed to look like murder. But—*how did you know,* Ballard? And Smith was drunk when he died. But—*how did you know,* Ballard? You weren't told that, Ballard."

Ballard looked at him a moment, dully. He shook his head, slowly.

"You'll never get away with it," he said. But there was no certainty in his voice. "You'd have to prove I stood to get something out of it and—"

"No," Heimrich said. "I wouldn't, actually. But, I can of course. That stood out all along. You all see that, surely. You do, don't you, Mr. Thayer?"

"The way I said," Arnold Thayer said, and there was no inflection in his voice. "There's no use trying to bring me into it. Nothing to do with me."

Ballard began to swear, then. He turned toward Thayer, and cursed him, and made as if to move toward him. But there were enough of them to stop him.

XV

THEY SAT AT a corner table on the porch of the Inn at Ridgefield. Heimrich sat at the end of the table, his back to West Lane; Wade Landcraft and Evelyn Merritt sat on his right, Harvey and Bonita at his left. He felt slightly paternal—at any rate avuncular. They finished *petites crêpes confiture,* drank *espresso* and were replete; the breeze under the awning was gentle, softly cool. "Worth the trip?" Harvey asked, having suggested it, and there were contented sighs. Bonita patted her husband's wrist and told him he had been very bright to think of it.

He assured her it had been nothing to think of—that they had all needed a deep breath of different air, needed an interval. "Out of the night that covered us," Bonita said and then looked across the table at Evelyn and did not say anything, but smiled at her. "Oh," Evelyn said, "I'm fine. I—" She looked at Wade, and there was something uncertain in her expression. Wade touched her hand.

"All the same," Evelyn said. "I should have known." She turned to the solid, blue-eyed man at the end of the table. She said, "You did, didn't you? Knew it wasn't Wade?"

Heimrich poured black-roasted coffee into a tiny cup,

twisted lemon peel over it, and drew deeply from his cigarette. Blue smoke from his lips floated over the chimneyed candles. He nodded his head.

"You said," Wade told him, "that it stood out all along."

Heimrich nodded again. He closed his eyes.

"Please, captain," Bonny Landcraft said. "Awake, for morning in the—"

"I don't," Harvey said, "know why I ever taught you to read."

It was often this way, Heimrich thought, and opened his eyes. Afterward, there was a flight to frivolity. The faces of the four still showed strain, and Evelyn's the most.

"You had no way of knowing, Miss Merritt," Heimrich said.

"You could have told me," she said. "But—you wanted—what? I suppose you thought I wouldn't be able to act. But—what difference did it make?"

"Now Miss Merritt," Heimrich said. "It helped. I wanted him to move. To make a mistake." He stubbed his cigarette out in an ash tray. "You were right, of course," he said, and spoke to Harvey Landcraft. "Miss Merritt couldn't have got away—from Ballard, from either of you, for that matter—unless she'd been let get away. That was obvious."

"Not to me," Evelyn said. "Oh—not to me, captain."

She had not been, Heimrich told her, in a position to consider with detachment. Ballard had been; when he had begun to argue that Evelyn's apparent escape had been real, he had begun to move.

"In other words," Bonny said, "you led him along. Gave him enough rope."

"Yes," Heimrich said. "In other words."

"And," Wade said, "already knew."

"Now Mr. Landcraft," Heimrich said. "I didn't see any other way things fitted—crime and character. I was fairly certain. But—I needed something overt. Unintentional admissions. Something like his attempt to attack Thayer, when he saw Thayer getting out from under." He lighted another cigarette. "Thayer probably will get out from under, incidentally," he said. "He's grown quite talkative, Mr. Thayer has. In an innocent way. The district attorney is pleased with him."

"Ballard's not talking, I suppose?" Harvey said. He was told that Ballard was not talking—yet. Not in the sense meant. He was being questioned. He was answering questions; answering many of them time after time. It was the usual thing, prompted by the usual necessities—the matters of time and place, of the specific how, the precise when; the details which filled out the picture, once you had the outline of the picture.

"You arrest first, get the evidence afterward," Harvey said, and added that it was very interesting.

"Now Mr. Landcraft," Heimrich said, and smiled faintly. "It's not quite that simple. But in a sense—yes, I suppose I do."

"It seems to me," Bonny said, "that you also invent evidence."

"Now Mrs. Landcraft," Heimrich said. "Let's say I arrange circumstances a little. Increase tensions a little. I wouldn't have taken the padlock matter into court, naturally."

"The defense will," Harvey said, and Heimrich shrugged. He said the defense might, if they thought it would help them. He said he doubted whether it would, since suicide was out, anyway—or a possibility too remote to be considered seriously.

They waited.

"Autopsy," Heimrich said. "Alcohol in the blood. High concentration—point forty something. Unless the man had great resistance, he was in a coma. He didn't have great resistance—we've checked on that. He was too drunk to kill himself. The defense will be reasonable doubt."

He did not continue. The reasonable doubt would be Wade Landcraft; there was no use bringing that up now, if it had been missed. He doubted it had. Well, it would worry them. That couldn't be helped.

"He won't get away with it?" Harvey asked and Heimrich said, "Oh, I shouldn't think so. The whole pattern's too much against him. Who else would frame the bull?"

Again they waited. He said it must be obvious; pointed out that he had already given them the outline, after Ballard's arrest the night before.

"I'm not sure," Wade Landcraft said, "that Evvie and I were—were listening very carefully." His hand was still on hers.

"No," Heimrich said. "Probably not. Well—for Ballard the method was a part of the motive. It wouldn't have been for anyone else—for either of you." He indicated the brothers. "Suppose you—or you—had wanted money badly enough to kill your mother to get it. Suppose one of you, or both of you together, had decided to kill her. Your purpose would have been to sell the herd, naturally. Get the cash. Naturally, you'd have wanted to sell as high as you could.

"So, you might have arranged an accident, or tried to. But—*the accident wouldn't have involved the bull.* You know enough about breeding, Wade, to know that that would bring his value down—bring the whole herd's value down. Perhaps not as much as Thayer wanted you to believe. It was to his advantage to exaggerate. But—nobody wants a mean bull. They breed mean.* Your whole interest would be to keep the value up.

"Ballard's interest was exactly opposite—to bring it down. That was his deal with Thayer—the way Thayer tells it, anyway. Thayer hinted enough when Crowley and I were talking to him to put me on the track. Not that the track wasn't pretty obvious anyway. Thayer says, now, that Ballard came to him and said, 'How'd you like to pick up Prince for twenty-five or thirty thousand?' Thayer says he just laughed, asked who wouldn't. 'O.K.,' he says Ballard said, 'if I can get him for you for that, do I get a half interest? Or—some sort of deal to breed heifers to him?' Thayer says he thought Ballard was having a pipe-dream, hadn't any idea what Ballard planned. Maybe he hadn't—then. He denies he ever did have. Well— Anyway, he doesn't deny he promised Ballard a deal—not a full share in the bull, he says, but 'a good deal.'

"So—Ballard killed Mrs. Landcraft. You can see how neat it looked. Kill her, and the herd would be sold off. Have the bull kill her, and the herd would sell cheap, the big bull particularly. He knew neither of you was interested in keeping the herd on, would want to get

* "Meanness and nervousness are inherent traits which are passed on to successive generations, greatly to the detriment of the herd."—Otto V. Battles, writing in "Cattle Raising at Its Best," a publication of the American Aberdeen-Angus Breeders' Association.

what cash you could, as soon as you could. I don't suppose you ever kept that from him?" The last was to Wade, who shook his head.

"Like that?" Evelyn said. "Just like that? In cold blood?"

"Yes," Heimrich said. "Of course, Ballard has a special feeling about the bull. He showed that when I first talked to him. The bull's sort of—well, sort of a dream to him. But, all the same, in cold blood."

"And Smith?" That was Bonita.

"I don't know," Heimrich said. "Probably Smith saw something—actually *didn't* see something, the scratch on Prince's leg."

"And the attack on Evvie?" That was Wade. "To throw it all on me, of course?"

"Naturally," Heimrich said. "Appear to try to silence her, let her get away so she could identify you as the man. Of course, we'd have suspected you anyway, because you were the only one she would have protected. Ballard thought of that."

Heimrich closed his eyes.

"He thought of a lot of things," he said. "Except—the one thing. Sitting tight." He was silent for a moment. "But then," he said, "that's characteristic, too. So many of them don't. You'd think—"

He opened his eyes. It occurred to him that he was not, any longer, being listened to with much attention. The four of them, now, had other things to think of.

So, Heimrich remembered, had he. He thought of sand and ocean.